Total Wheelspin

The author Tony Davis is a popular newspaper columnist and has written more than a dozen books for adults and children. These include *Wide Open Road*, the companion book to the ABC television series, and *The Big Dry*, a dystopian novel aimed at younger readers (HarperCollins). He maintains a fascination with anything that moves, and the stranger it is, the better.

Total
Wheelspin

Car culture, quizzes, myths and motoring madness

TONY DAVIS

ABC
Books

The ABC 'Wave' device is a trademark of the
Australian Broadcasting Corporation and is used
under licence by HarperCollins*Publishers* Australia.

First published in Ausralia in 2013
by HarperCollins*Publishers* Australia Pty Limited
ABN 36 009 913 517
harpercollins.com.au

HarperCollins*Publishers*
Level 13, 201 Elizabeth Street, Sydney NSW Australia
31 View Road, Glenfield, Auckland 0627, New Zealand
A 53, Sector 57, Noida, UP, India
77–85 Fulham Palace Road, London W6 8JB, United Kingdom
2 Bloor Street East, 20th floor, Toronto, Ontario M4W 1A8, Canada
10 East 53rd Street, New York NY 10022, USA

National Library of Australia Cataloguing-in-Publication entry:

Davis, Tony.
Total wheelspin/ Tony Davis.
978 0 7333 3289 0 (pbk.)
978 1 4607 0169 0 (ebook)
Automobiles – Driving – Humor.
Automobiles – Humor.
Australian Broadcasting Corporation.
629.2220207

Cover design by Hazel Lam, HarperCollins Design Studio
Front cover image: Another mad micro — the 1959 British-made Scootacar (wheelspin not pictured). Photo
by Darin Schnabel/RM Auctions (rmauctions.com)
Printed and bound in the U.S.A. by RR Donnelley

5 4 3 2 1   14 15 16

Acknowledgments

Thanks to those at ABC Books (especially Brigitta Doyle, Jennifer Blau and Helen Cooney) who worked on this project, and to those at Fairfax Media who have published my musings on cars over the years – even when they have become very, very odd.

Photo Credits: Photos are from Marque Publishing or the author's private collection except for those on the following pages:

- From RM Auctions (rmauctions.com). Photographer: Darin Schnabel: Cover photo, 37, 83, 254, 255 (both shots).
- From Vic Fearn & Company Ltd (crazycoffins.co.uk): 87, 89.
- From Dr John Wright: 124.
- From Wikimedia Commons: 5, 19, 46 (Joe Mabel), 50 (Matthias v.d. Elbe), 55, 63, 65, 85, 102, 111, 113, 132, 144 (Alexander Plushev), 146, 155 (Buch-t), 164, 166, 176 (Matthew Reichbach), 177 (Sage Ross), 179, 183 (Sam Howzit), 186 and back cover (Jennifer Graylock/Ford), 189 (Wammes Waggel), 208, 219 (Sicnag), 221, 236 (Andy7764, top, and Chris Keating, bottom), 287, 289, 290, 292 (Maujak), 307 (Wing-Chi Poon), 308 (Juliancolton)

Note on the text: *Total Wheelspin* combines work published in *The Sydney Morning Herald*, *The Age* and other sources with new and updated material.

Contents

Introduction

Total Wheelspin is a car book with a difference – the difference being that it explores those areas of the automotive world that rarely get a look in.

Whether it's the weirdest and most mysterious cars ever built, would-be automobile magnates who dress as women and star on 'America's Most Wanted', racing drivers who are champions at talking drivel, or the favourite cars of dictators, *Total Wheelspin* puts on the pith helmet and khaki shorts, raises the binoculars and takes the exploration metaphor further than others dare.

The text is presented under such headings as:

Technicalities – Can you power your car with water? When will flying cars go on sale? And here's the truth about those absolutely proven inventions that are still being suppressed – miracle carburettor, anyone?

On human nature – Why do we behave like we do behind the wheel? Why do we buy the strange machines we buy, and who the hell decided hanging one arm out the window is a fashion statement?

Cars of the world – Not just the obscure, but the very obscure too. And the oddball. The *très* oddball. Plus the real reason ultra-conservatives shun Mazdas and hybrids.

Historical notes – From the origins of road rage through to the

Carriage of presidents: 1952 Cadillac Eldorado and Dwight D. Eisenhower.

Bending the rules: France's leaning Lumeneo Smera.

The Citroen DS returns as an art installation in Paris.

Top flight Americana: the 1963 Corvette.

world's jammiest traffic jams. And at last: a list of the ways cigarette companies have done the right thing by motorists.

Based on a true story – This is a Hollywood expression meaning 'almost entirely invented'. In this spirit, these entries can be a little loose with the truth. Small lies, though, can reveal big truths. Or even bigger lies.

Frequently unasked questions – Why are safety recalls explained the way they are, and not the way they should be? Who is shaping the language of brochures and PR … could it really be someone named Fifi?

Men and machines – Eccentrics, innovators and despots, some of

whom have built cars, others who merely drive or smash them. All we need to know about Colonel Gaddafi's Rocket car, plus a bit we don't.

Motoring culture – Books and films: who could ignore the Australian classic *My Love Had a Black Speed Stripe*? Or fail to ignore *Redline*, possibly the worst film about cars (or anything else) ever made?

Rattletraps, etc. – A return to a favourite subject (shockingly bad machines), though with some new twists. And more cars from British Leyland. What about bad German cars, though? Yep, got that covered.

Let's get quizzical – Test your motoring knowledge in the safety of your own home. You can't be sure when knowing the connection between Japanese cars and the ancient Persian religion of Zoroastrianism will come in handy.

Breaking these topics up are short **interludes** filled entirely with four-wheeled falsehoods. These pay tribute to all those Internet motoring trivia sites that get most things wrong. Why restrict yourself to half-truths when you can go all the way? Enjoy.

Tony Davis
Sydney, Australia 2013

1 Can I power my car with water?

Of course you can. Don't you read your email spam file? You can add inches while you're at it ... and what about helping that nice Nigerian man with his banking difficulties?

Cynics disagree. But then, they have to. It's part of their job description.

They say that extracting net energy from water contradicts the principles of thermodynamics and that, in general terms, running a car on water will work only downhill, and at the expense of your engine.

This is a very glum view when there are so many advantages of trying to tap (so to speak) the most wonderfully plentiful fuel supply in the world.

Think how well placed we'd be down here in Australia with 26,000 kilometres of coastline. And wouldn't anyone who'd paid a premium for a hybrid look like a wally?

Sadly, though, the cynics might be right.

Here's a typical spiel from carthatrunsonwater.net: 'This 90-year-old technology has finally escaped the grips of those who held it a secret. ... This modification device can pay for itself within 30 days ... It will NOT void your Auto Warranty and can actually add years to the life of your enigne.'

Who can say they haven't wanted to add years to the life of their *enigne*?

Cars claiming to use water as fuel gain most prominence when there is a spike in the price of oil. David Mamet's 1977 play, *The Water Engine,* was about a young man who invented just that and became the victim of all types of skulduggery.

In the 1980s, Stanley Meyer, an American, garnered huge publicity with his miracle dune buggy. He had replaced the spark plugs with, er, water plugs. These sprayed a fine mist into the cylinders, which was subjected to a certain electrical something which broke the H_2O into H_2 and O and … blah blah blah … buy shares today or you'll miss out.

Meyer's technology was so radical, and his enemies so vociferous, he couldn't safely subject his vehicle to independent testing, lest someone steal his concepts.

To his many admirers, Meyer's later convictions for investor fraud were proof of how hard the government and other dark forces were trying to stifle him. And when he died suddenly in 1998, it was obvious he had been poisoned by agents of the military-industrial-petroleum complex.

A story entitled 'Burning water and other myths' showed that the supposedly respected magazine *Nature* was also in on the conspiracy to discredit the water engine. In a September 2007 edition, Philip Ball wrote:

It's not easy to establish how Meyer's car was meant to work, except that it involved a fuel cell that was able to split water using less energy than was released by recombination of the elements … [but] water is not a fuel. It never has been one, and it never will be one. Water does not burn … it is spent fuel. It is exhaust.

Genepax is one of many cars that run on water. Or don't.

Ball lamented that 'the myth of water as a fuel is never going to go away'. Certainly in 2006 we had America's Denny Klein, whose 1994 Ford Escort could drive '100 miles on 4 ounces of water'. Such 'inventions' inspire near-hysterical press, often from very blonde newsreaders.

'He has already attracted the attention of an unnamed American automaker,' reported one-such, 'and Klein has been invited to Washington to demonstrate his technology, with word that he is now working on a water–gasoline hybrid Hummer for the US military.'

In mid-2008 Japan's Genepax company unveiled a car that could convert water to electrical power. There was similar media excitement: 1 litre was enough to propel it for a whole hour at 80 km/h! Yet not a word since. Must be a conspiracy.

2 The English assortment

So, what have those folks in Blighty done for us? The immediate answer is 'plenty'. They gave us the E-Type Jaguar, the Mini, the Morris Minor, the Aston-Martin DB-5.

They also served the Austin Seven, the Lotus-Cortina, the MG TC, some wonderful pre-war Rileys, Le Mans-winning Bentleys and the Rolls-Royce brand.

Plus the McLaren F1! This superbly wrought technological powerhouse deserved to be released in something other than a global financial meltdown (that of the early 1990s) and see its total production restricted to little more than a hundred.

Jaguar's spectacular E-Type.

The Austin Allegro, popularly known as the 'all aggro'.

Who wouldn't want an Austin-Healey 3000?

On the other hand, who *would* want an Austin Allegro, arguably the most reviled and lampooned mainstream car of all time, or a Jensen-Healey, perhaps the most unreliable.

Or a Jaguar XJ220 – the porkiest, flabbiest, most unwanted-iest supercar of them all?

It was Rudyard Kipling who wrote, 'If you can meet with Triumph and Disaster, and treat those two impostors just the same … you'll be a Man, my son!'

If he'd ever driven a Stag, Herald, or Mayflower, The Kipster would have known that Triumph and Disaster can be one and the same thing.

The English built an almost endless series of Bonds, Reliants and other highly lamentable mini-cars. They lacked go. They lacked stop. They even lacked sideways.

The bigger Daimler Dart can also be parked neatly in the 'Indefensible' column. Slightly less hideous than a lobster with acne scars, this plastic-bodied roadster displayed such a lack of structural

Fit for Bond: the Aston-Martin DB-5.

rigidity the doors popped open under hard cornering. How did the same country – only a few years later – build the Jensen Interceptor FF, a svelte all-wheel-drive V8 sports car with antilock brakes? In 1967!

Or so many wonderful, innovative eccentricities? Take the motorcycle-engined Rocket of the 1990s. I certainly would. Largely designed by Gordon Murray, this tandem two-seater was styled like a 1960s Cooper F1 car and was light, fast, tactile and everything a great sports car should be. Except successful enough to keep the company afloat.

Yep, good and bad. But there's one thing the English have produced more of than anyone else: cars on both sides of the ledger. Which is to say, cars that passionately polarise enthusiasts.

Even the Triumph Stag has a small but fervent coterie of admirers. Likewise the MGB, unveiled at the Earls Court Motor Show in 1962. The official fiftieth anniversary celebrations in the UK opened and closed with static showcases at Blenheim Palace.

There are those who might say static showcases – ideally on highly absorbent grass – are entirely appropriate considering the car's atrocious reliability.

Others will say that such a comment is exactly the sort of cheap shot you'd expect from an arrogant, Pommy-bashing ignoramus. And such people are perfectly entitled to hold that opinion, no matter how wrong it is.

Maybe the original Lotus Elan is the best example of contradictory English endeavour. It was filled with fresh thinking, looked great and was acclaimed by many as the world's best-handling sports car.

Yet buying one took equal parts bravery, stupidity and financial imprudence.

From 1970, the all-wheel-drive Range Rover set new standards for stranding people in hard-to-get-to places. When its growing reputation for English build quality was countered with a series of long-distance records set by 'specially modified' examples, one suspected the modifications were specifically aimed at removing anything Range Rover.

The Rangie somehow survived. The Jensen Interceptor didn't. Indeed, the Jensen achieved the rare feat of sending its builder broke not just on one occasion, but several.

The vast majority of other British brands are also defunct. The ones that are still funct are mostly that way due to overseas help. Still, most countries would be proud if they'd produced a small fraction as much.

3 Why the arm out the window?

There are several major trends one can note in recent years: environmentalism, the rise of social media, evangelical atheism and people driving cars with their right arm permanently hanging out the window.

The people – OK, males – involved in this last trend are not simply hanging their arms out the window. They are doing it in a very specific and, I think, twenty-first century way.

The elbow is hooked over the windowsill, the arm swings limply, nonchalantly, while the thumb rubs the paintwork.

There is obviously a message being conveyed, though its exact nature is hard to divine.

It could be 'My door won't close properly, but I'm going to hold it only half-heartedly.' It may be 'I need only one arm to do what the rest of you think needs two.' Or, and I think this is perhaps the strongest possibility, 'I am a complete and utter moron who should have been drowned at birth.' Let's look at the pros and cons of this surprisingly popular driving style. Firstly, the car produces slightly more drag with the window open. If there's air-conditioning, it works less efficiently. It is noisier inside as well as hotter. Or colder.

More importantly than these, the total number of upper limbs available for controlling a tonne or two of steel is reduced by, broadly speaking, 50 per cent. The blinker is rarely used and the classic ten-to-two driving position becomes one hand on the nine.

And the pros? Well, you can impress people who are impressed by people who hang their arms out of cars.

The limb that isn't being pressed into service is also highly exposed. In addition to all of the above, this exposure leads some people – all right, me – to occasionally, fleetingly, entertain the fantasy of swerving just enough to … splat!

Anyway, such admissions are diverting us from a serious discussion on the Millsian notion of liberty, and whether 'over himself, over his own body and mind, the individual is sovereign'. Does the rule book support Mr John Stuart Mill's notion and say that if you want to expose a limb

– perhaps hang your foot out the bottom of the door through a special doggy flap instead – then it's none of the government's business?

Rule 268 in the New South Wales Road Rules suggests not. The statutes in other states are probably similar, but you can't expect a grumpy old man to read through more than one.

New South Wales declares: 'A person must not travel in or on a motor vehicle with any part of the person's body outside a window or door of the vehicle, unless the person is the driver of the vehicle and is giving a hand signal: (a) for changing direction to the right in accordance with rule 50, or (b) for stopping or slowing in accordance with rule 55.'

There are a few other exceptions in the small print, but absolutely no provision for hand signals designed to show other road-users that your head is entirely filled with McDonald's-grade hamburger mince.

Which is a pity, since such information might be more useful to other road-users than the mere fact that your car is going to change direction or stop.

On the other hand (which can't be as easily hung out the window of an Australian car), Mill argued society could intervene if potential self-harm could lead to the harm of others, which is why he'd probably say, 'Pull the arm in, mate, but make your own mind up about the seat belt.'

Mill himself never wore a seatbelt, though that was less to do with his ground-breaking views on liberty than the fact he died in 1873.

4 The truth about racing films

They're not very good, are they?

It's hard to work out why. Adding a car chase is the standard way to enliven a dull police procedural, or pretty well any other filmed entertainment.

So why not have the whole movie a car chase? Better still, why not have scriptwriters compress into ninety minutes everything a typical motor-racing season delivers: speed, thrills, spills, politics, adultery, espionage, skulduggery, ugly short men and beautiful women?

How can even Hollywood mess that up? Well, for a start by falling into monumental cliché. Let's look at the plot summary (from IMDB) of the 1932 James Cagney movie *The Crowd Roars*:

> Famous motor-racing champion Joe Greer returns to his hometown to compete … He discovers his younger brother has aspirations to become a racing champion and during the race Joe loses his nerve when another driver is killed, leaving his brother to win. Joe's luck takes a plunge whilst his brother rises to the height of fame.

Then let's look at Sylvester Stallone's notoriously bad 2001 effort, *Driven,* or, as it is more popularly known, *Drivel.*

NOTHING STOPS "THE RACERS"...

A love story that hurtles full speed across the barriers of convention...
in Paris, Rome, Monte Carlo, Nice, The Swiss Alps!

THE RACERS

Color by DE LUXE

from
20th Century-Fox in CinemaScope

In the Wonder of
STEREOPHONIC
SOUND

KIRK DOUGLAS · BELLA DARVI · GILBERT ROLAND

CESAR ROMERO · KATY JURADO · LEE J. COBB

with Charles Goldner
George Dolenz

Produced by JULIAN BLAUSTEIN · Directed by HENRY HATHAWAY · Screen play by CHARLES KAUFMAN

S I G N A T U R E

Talented rookie Jimmy Bly ... begins to slip in the race rankings. It's no wonder, with the immense pressure being shovelled on him by his overly ambitious promoter brother as well as Bly's romance with his arch-rival's girlfriend Sophia. ... Former racing star Joe Tanto [is recruited] to help [but he] must first deal with the emotional scars left over from a tragic racing accident, which nearly took his life.

Somewhere between those two plots (or lack thereof) is the basis of almost every fictional racing film.

Steve McQueen's film *Le Mans* from 1971 broke the mould, in that it had even less happening. The opening scenes are so languid they are reminiscent of the TV series 'Brideshead Revisited'. ('BR' is twenty years in the life of a stately English home, filmed in real time.)

Le Mans goes for thirty-eight minutes before any real dialogue is spoken: a very short exchange between McQueen and the widow of another driver.

The widow is one cliché, but some others are avoided. When a driver promises his wife he'll retire at the end of the race, you have to think, 'This is not a good move if you want to survive the film.'

As it turns out, that driver isn't killed in a fireball, and McQueen – the hero, of course, and an American, of double-course – neither wins the race nor beds the girl.

Lack of story aside, *Le Mans* is a beautifully shot portrait of sports car racing in 1970 – so realistic and hard-edged it's surprising anyone thought there'd be a general market (there wasn't much of one).

Although spoken lines are few, they include the usual sensible woman bemoaning the danger. McQueen's response is equally unoriginal. 'When you're racing, it's life. Anything that happens before or after is just waiting.'

That's yet another variation on the line attributed to Karl Wallenda, the tightrope-walking patriarch of the Flying Wallendas circus act. He said, 'Life is on the wire, everything else is waiting.' Wallenda lived the maxim too, slipping off a wire fatally in 1978. He was aged seventy-three, and probably cursing that thief McQueen as he fell.

5 What do old buggers say?

You like it, mate? Did it up myself. Bare metal, stripped down to the last nut and bolt.

It's a rare one, of course. They only ever built twelve examples with the five-speed and four-barrel; only one in this colour.

Probably priceless but I'd never sell it because, well, the sentimental value.

I worked on the line, way back then. Well, I wasn't just a line worker, I was a bit higher up than that. Surprised you don't recognise me, you being a car bloke and all that.

Here's my card. See the name … no, still doesn't ring a bell? Oh well, *sic transit gloria* and all that, but geez I could tell you some stories.

You're in a hurry? That's OK, but I didn't just work at Ford and Holden, you know. I was a safety engineer at Chrysler Australia. And you know that first run of Valiants in 1962? Here's something you could write about: every one of them had a driver-side airbag.

We designed it all locally, along with an engine powered by milk, but that's another story. The managing director – some silly American named Chip or something – said he never wanted safety devices because they reminded people of car crashes.

So we had to remove the sensors. But even now if you take off the horn button from those cars you'll find the airbag underneath. Might be a bit sticky now – it was made of natural rubber and, in the first tests, it did jettison the horn ring with such force it punched a perfect donut in the test dummy.

But imagine if we had the support to develop it properly?

No, come back, just for a minute. I'll tell you real quick about Ferrari of Ballarat. Yes, Ballarat. I'm always amazed by the things people don't know. During the late 1960s most Ferraris were built there. There were too many strikes in Italy, and the Mafia took a cut on each car built.

A bunch of former Italian prisoners of war had the idea. I helped set up the production line with a few ex-Chrysler guys. We banged them together in this big shed where they once built World War II bombers.

Shipped them back to The Continent at the end so they could rivet on a plaque saying 'Made in Italy'. It was true: that's where the plaque was made.

Don't go, that's just reminded me of something else. You'd be interested in motor sport, wouldn't you? Remember the XU-1 Torana? That was something else I was involved in, in a modest sort of way.

I sketched the design on the leg of my overalls during the rather long wait between each Ferrari because, well, they weren't exactly a mass-produced item.

General Motors began building them – they made a few changes to my design, admittedly – and the next thing you know they're saying 'You're the guy who set all those records at Mallala Raceway, aren't you?' and asking if I'd drive for them.

Ended up winning Bathurst seven times but, you know how these things happen, I had to wear a full-face Peter Brock mask for sponsorship reasons.

I kept the prize money, though. That was enough, as I've never been one to big-note myself. And, hey, I was a bit bored with racing by that stage, so I let Peter have a go.

He wasn't a bad driver, and he did win a couple of times in his own right toward the end, once I'd agreed to hand-build his engines and run his pit-crew. He wanted me to design and build his HDT road-cars too, but …

Hey, it's getting a bit hard to shout, with you standing so far away. Did I tell you about the Escort hybrid I built when I was head of engineering at Ford, or the time I …

6 Caution: falling magnates

We all secretly dream of being a motoring magnate, don't we? You know, with cars sliding sideways across the road and sticking to us.

OK, maybe not that sort of magnate. The type with our surname on the grille. Hell, we want a city built around our firm and a shining glass tower for a head office, topped with a logo that can be seen from space.

We want our car to be a byword for quality, innovative design, stylishness and impossibly impressive performance.

That's not too much to ask, is it? Well, talk to the thousands who have tried and lost their shirt, often without selling even a single car. Even those who did make it, and saw their name in lights – or on lights (and steering wheels and boot lids) – haven't always spent their dotage lapping up champagne and praise.

Who and how? Here are a few examples …

The man born William Crapo Durant, better known as Billy Durant, had a career that seemed to follow the trajectory of a restored vintage jet fighter taking its maiden flight at a crowded air show, as seen on grainy newsreel footage in the documentary *Aviation Carnage*.

Durant formed General Motors, lost control of it, co-founded Chevrolet and used its success to merge his way back into control of GM, then managed to throw all that away too. He founded Durant cars, made a fortune on Wall Street, lost that too, and ended up running the 'Bowl-a-Rama Billy' bowling alley in Michigan.

Louis Chevrolet did even worse. The car-builder-cum-racing-driver ended up an assembly line worker at Chevrolet, the company he had started with Durant.

Kim Woo-choong's high point? Circa 1997, when he was the founder and boss not just of Daewoo cars but of the whole Daewoo colossus, with twenty major divisions making everything from handguns to oil tankers. He was also author of the 'inspiring autobiography' entitled *It's a big world, and there's a lot to be done*.

Woo-choong's low point was fleeing the country shortly after, with Daewoo collapsing under a debt of more than $50 billion. On coming out of hiding in 2005, he was sentenced to ten years in jail and fined a kazillion won. The president eventually pardoned him, though his book had long since been remaindered.

W.O. Bentley built cars that won Le Mans and were *the* thing to have for the well-to-do Englishman-about-town. But W.O. couldn't make money and his company fell into the hands of rival Rolls-Royce. In his later years Bentley drove a Morris Minor, insisting he couldn't afford one of the cars he'd designed and built.

Louis Chevrolet, when still smiling.

John Delorean's high point was either being the blue-eyed boy at GM, the man behind the Pontiac GTO (and, soon after, the head of the Pontiac division, then Chevrolet) or, perhaps, bringing his own car to market in 1981.

The ego of the man is shown by the car's name: Delorean DMC-12. The DMC stood for Delorean Motor Company, enabling him to squeeze in his own name twice. The car itself, of course, was a dog with fleas and a financial black hole.

The low point for Delorean was his arrest while setting up a cocaine deal to rescue the car company. He was acquitted on grounds of entrapment, but died penniless.

Henry Ford died in 1947. Toward the end, he lit his house with candles to save money, even though he had more than $26 million in the bank.

In the 1920s and 1930s Louis Renault was supreme boss of a highly successful car company so megalomaniacal it built everything, even the bricks to build its factories. In 1944, he was jailed by his compatriots as an alleged Nazi collaborator, and fatally beaten.

Yep, that's how far you can fall.

John Delorean, after failing to close those silly doors.

7 The other Germans

Germans as a rule don't build bad cars. But when they drop the ball, boy does it hit the ground hard. Here are some Teutonic low points:

Trabant P601 – OK, a bit obvious. But it was *the* four-wheeled symbol of a system that didn't work. There were similar cars produced on the Western side of the wall in the early 1960s, such as the Goggomobil, but the Westerners stopped making them as soon as they became more affluent. The Easties never got to that point and their cars were frozen in time – a noisy, two-stroke time at that.

BMW 3-Series Compact – You know, the first hatch they did, in the mid-1990s. Looked like they did it by just lopping the boot off the standard model. Buyers may as well have declared 'I couldn't afford a whole BMW but they agreed to sell me five-sixths of one.'

NSU RO 80 – This curious, high-tailed, last gasp from NSU could also be in the list of best German cars. With a Wankel engine and a long list of other innovations, it was an ambitious recipe. If it had spent longer in the oven it might not have brought so much expensive trouble and so many smoky breakdowns.

Mercedes SL (R107) – There are some – me, for instance – who consider the 'pagoda roof' SL of the 1960s one of the most lithe and graceful cars ever built. Then Benz applied the Mustang formula, which insists that each iteration must be bigger, heavier and uglier

The Schwein Class.

than the one before. Hence 1972's fat-arsed replacement. There was something worse – the stretched wheelbase SLC hardtop, which had the same corpulent looks but more of them, and underlined its complete pointlessness by preventing you from taking the roof off.

Porsche Cayenne – Why? Why? Why? For the bucks, of course. This re-skinned Veedub with a Porsche price tag made so much lucre they immediately started work on a smaller version called Macan. Presumably as in 'macan quick money while trashing brand values'.

Wartburg – Another smoky Eastern-Bloc shocker, not as well known as the Trabant, but nigh as nasty. Three-cylinder two-stroke engine, frumpy styling, odious build quality … you get the picture. The company lasted about thirty seconds once the wall came down.

Mercedes-Benz S Class (W140) – Known to some as the Schwein Class, the 1991 model was bloated and outrageously heavy. It was a superb technological achievement in many ways, but was completely wrong for the lean times that hit the market just after it did.

BMW M6 – Take a big four-wheel drive with its centre of gravity just below the clouds and restyle it so that it looks laughable and has the packaging efficiency of a 1-Series on stilts. Add a huge engine and low-profile tyres, and drop the suspension so it can't be taken off road. The result? The answer to a question no sensible person would ask.

Maybach 57 – It looked like a Hyundai Grandeur that had been put on the rack. It was named after a supposedly prestigious car not even Germans could remember and was priced like a Rolls-Royce competitor. Which almost nobody thought it was. The Maybach 62 was worse. Five worse.

VW Phaeton – So, some great lummox decided VW should take on the S-Class Benz with something offering better value for money. D'oh! When was value for money part of the consideration with S-Class Benz buyers? And when did they want a 'people's car' badge?

Heinkel Kabine – Take this entry as covering the Isetta, Messerschmitt, Zundapp Janus and those other ludicrously proportioned, flagrantly unstable cabin scooters and micro cars. But comes a time to forgive and forget! Anyone can make a mistake. Or two.

Heinkel Cabine.

8 How are recalls explained?

Very quietly. Whereas motor vehicle brochures are 100 per cent hyperbole, recall notices are the opposite. They use words that are dull, neutral and vague to downplay any unpleasant consequences. Such as death, to choose one example.

Take Fiat's explanation of a potentially loose Punto component that '... could eventually break with consequences on the steering direction control'. Now, don't know about you, but I'm quite fond of steering direction control. If there's a real and present danger of if going south, it would be nice to be told about it in good old-fashioned clear English.

Something like: 'The steering might fracture, rupture or shatter and, if it does, matie, you're ...'

The early Ferrari 458s had problems with 'thermal incidents'. Anyone who speaks fluent recall will know that a thermal incident can involve large flames and a charred wreck at the end.

Fortunately, the purpose of a recall is sound enough – to fix a problem, sorry, issue before any owners or bystanders are sliced, diced or flambéed.

The system usually works. All Australian Ferrari 458s, for example, were lassoed and dragged in to correct the 'possible non-conformity in the assembly of the wheelhouse and its respective heat shield'. Owners, each of whom have paid more than half a mill for their 458, must have been reassured to learn that it was a 'non-conformity' rather than, say, a mistake, stuff-up or quality lapse.

Land Rover told its owners that, in the case of the Defender, 'full windshield retention may not be achieved in the event of a crash of sufficient severity to deploy the front airbags'. How about a bit of plain speaking, Mr L. Rover? How about 'Hit something hard and you can expect your glassware to end up in a different postcode.'

Mind you, the current Defender is only a minor update of the model that came out on the First Fleet. I didn't realise it had airbags; I assumed a hand came out of the dashboard, slapped you around and told you to man up.

Bentley, in typical circumlocutory recall fashion, revealed potential problems with the Arnage bonnet mascot. The statement underscored another major difference between recall notices and brochures.

'There is the potential,' Bentley affirmed, 'for the retractable "B" mechanism to become corroded. In extreme cases, this may lead to the flying "B" mascot not retracting when struck, [causing] additional injury in the event of a pedestrian impact.'

Notice not just the blatant understatement, but also the apparent disinterest in using a golden opportunity to stress brand values and key marketing messages. Why don't car makers get their brochure writers to do recall notices too? Or, to put it another way, why can't such a declaration be written in the sort of language that would make Bentley owners take notice, and would reinforce that, despite such minor problems, they've made the right choice? Here's a humble suggestion:

'Owners of the majestic Bentley Arnage are no strangers to the cut and thrust of business and sharp negotiations. Many of them are now taking that leading edge to the street.

'In extreme cases, the iconic "Flying B" bonnet mascot – this renowned symbol of engineering excellence, this hallmark of power and sporting prowess, this distinguished sculptural representation of the first letter of founder W.O. Bentley's surname, as worn with pride atop radiator grilles during four consecutive Le Mans victories – may disembowel sluggish pedestrians.

'They could leave their entrails over the distinguished, craftsman-built bodywork, finished in your choice of 114 deep and lustrous colours, each of which can be matched to twenty-four sumptuous interior hides and a dozen superbly grained wood veneers.'

Just a thought. It would certainly make the ACCC's Product Safety Recalls website a more lively read.

9 A short rundown on road rage

The term road rage has only been with us since about 1988, apparently, but the rage itself seems to go way back, at least as far as the earliest cars.

There are even reports from the days of the horse and buggy, with one Henry Morris being fined £12 in 1850 for deliberately crashing into a cart he was overtaking on the road to Nottingham.

He yelled to the other driver, 'I'll cut your pony's head off if you come nigh me.'

Road rage is not just cursing under your breath that everyone else on the road is a freaking idiot who is trying to kill you – which is not entirely unreasonable because, as we all know, everyone else on the road is a freaking idiot who is trying to kill you.

It implies acting on your anger. The research paper *Controlling Road Rage: A Literature Review and Pilot Study* defines it as 'an incident in which an angry or impatient motorist or passenger intentionally injures or kills another motorist, passenger, or pedestrian, or attempts or threatens to injure or kill another motorist, passenger, or pedestrian'. Meanwhile, Leon James and Diane Nahl, authors of *Road Rage and Aggressive Driving*, define aggressive driving as the desire to impose one's own level of risk on others and to force others to drive according to one's own standards.

But AD can easily lead to RR. If you effect violent lane changes and *you're-not-going-to-overtake-me-you-bastard* bursts of acceleration, physical or metallic violence will likely follow.

Road rage gets a mention in America's big book of official medical definitions, the *Diagnostic and Statistical Manual of Mental Disorders* (DSM). It comes under a category known as Intermittent Explosive Disorder.

Therefore, that person stoving in your head with a tyre iron because you were doing 59 km/h in a single-lane sixty zone is not a vicious creep, but the victim of an illness and deserving of your pity. Even if that pity has to be afforded posthumously.

If road rage truly is a disease, or a control disorder, the phenomenon has probably always been there, and cars just give us another way of expressing it. It's a particularly dangerous way of expressing it. When you kick a printer or photocopier, the only victim is an inanimate machine that almost certainly deserves it. But when you have a tonne or two of machinery under your direct control ...

Surprisingly, one of the best commentaries comes not from a legal or medical source, but from Disney. *Motor Mania* is an animated short made in 1950, long before the term road rage was coined. Goofy is mild-mannered 'Mr Walker' who can stop and smell the flowers on foot. When in his car, though, he turns into mad-as-a-cut-snake 'Mr Wheeler'. The voice-over explains that, once he has steering wheel in hand and accelerator underfoot, he 'is charged with an overwhelming sense of power ... his whole personality changes, abruptly he becomes an uncontrollable monster'. That's understating it; Mr Wheeler is an outright psychopath, screaming at

other motorists, racing them at every opportunity, sideswiping and ramming cars he considers not fast enough, blocking others when he himself feels like slowing down.

He punches the steering wheel at a red light, bemoaning the thirty seconds of his life that has been lost, and swerves across the road towards a puddle so he can splash a pedestrian loaded down with shopping bags. OK, we've all done that last one, haven't we? Just joking …

The thing is that Mr Walker's own experiences as a pedestrian – he's shown with barking cars chasing him up a light-pole at one point – don't seem to register at all when the roles are reversed.

In that sense, *Motor Mania* is just like real life. And it makes you angry. Really, really angry. No, I mean furious …

10 When will our flying cars be ready?

The lack of a flying car in your driveway is a massive breach of trust. Flying cars were one of the things we, as consumers, were specifically promised by the year 2000.

This firm and binding assurance was delivered via thousands of magazine articles, television documentaries and learned papers by futurists. And we've been let down time and time again.

The flying car is almost as old as the non-flying. The first auto-with-wings was patented in 1918 and, like most of those that would follow, it failed to fly soon afterwards.

Dozens and dozens have been unveiled since, ranging from the unsuccessful to the unbelievable. If most of them were pies, they simply wouldn't rise high enough to be pies in the sky. Canadian inventor Dr Paul Moller took the first deposit on one of his vertical take-off, bubble-roofed, family-sized Skycars in the 1970s. He still hasn't delivered and, frankly, neither has anyone else.

At least Dr Moller's vehicles look high-tech. The Magic Dragon – which has been in development even longer – has a big squared-off nose and crude bolt-on wings.

The man behind this flying FJ Holden, 'retired Air Force Command

Pilot-Aero Engineer' Richard Strong, promised a few years ago that deliveries 'may begin' in 2010.

Yep, just after world peace is achieved, along with a cure for all known diseases.

The Skybike from Sampson Motorworks in California is a streamliner with pop-out wings. It looks like it fell out of a *Popular Mechanics* magazine from 1972. Sales would start in late 2009, we were told, falsely. And initially as a kit.

A kit! If there's one thing less likely to fly than a flying car, it's surely a flying car built out of a cardboard box in the guy-down-the-street's garage.

Australia's Sky Bike adds a propeller and wings to any motorbike of 250 cc or more. The makers claim you can even take your pillion up into the air. If anyone wants to offer me a ride, unfortunately I'm doing something else that day.

England's Parajet Sky Car is just as curious: a dune buggy that sits beneath a ramjet-style parachute. A big fan blows it along. I'm busy that day too.

At least this 'flying car' is playing it for laughs.

The LaBiche, from Texas, could be mistaken for an amateurish fibreglass replica of a 1970s Le Mans racer, except there are slots all over the bodywork. These are so the eight wings can suddenly *boing!* out at the appropriate moment.

Israel's Urban Aeronautics is working on a snazzy, helicoptery car that will supposedly hover above roads and swerve between buildings. An unmanned prototype has actually taken off, but the 2010 launch date came and went.

One of the better funded projects is the Terrafugia Transition, 'a roadable Light Sport Aircraft designed by a team of award-winning MIT-trained engineers for today's demanding general aviation pilot'. Another is the PAL-V, a European three-wheeled gyrocopter.

Both look promising, but then 'promising' is a flying car company speciality. Unlike, say, 'taking off' or 'being delivered to customers now'. Still, as long as there are no flying cars, there'll be no rock-apes hovering above your house playing doof doof music, or P-platers racing on public airways, or three-dimensional traffic jams.

And school mums won't be clamouring for flying 4WDs, so it can't be all bad.

11 Lies, big and small

Lies, big and small, circulate in cyberspace and on good old-fashioned paper. Perhaps it's because people believe what they want to believe. Or maybe it's because if something is repeated often enough, it becomes a fact. Even if it's so obviously an unfact, such as:

- Despite its name, the original Audi quattro – the acclaimed five-cylinder turbocharged coupe from 1980 – drove only three wheels. The other wheel was used for braking.
- Belgium's only completely homegrown car, the Doldrum GT, was financed by Belgian-French singer Johnny Hallyday with the royalties from his hit song 'Le Rock, Le Roll, Le Groovy Groovy Yeah-Yeah-Yeah'. The car, like the song, lost pretty well everything in the translation.
- Double-clutch transmissions are illegal in Mali, Togo and three other northern African countries on religious grounds.
- Soichiro Honda's middle name was Edgar. His younger sisters were Doreen and Gladys.
- In the nineteen-year gap between the launch of the Ford Model T and its replacement, the Model A, Henry Ford became restless and built the prototype for 'a transportable communication device that would produce a variety of different ringtones and also enable you

to play Solitaire'. It was said to be small enough to fit wholly within the tray of a small utility truck.

- The outer panels of the original Maybach 62 were made from Boglar, a light, strong and ultra-expensive composite material taking in high-tech polymers, titanium and Irish peat.

- Aston-Martin was named after a vaudeville act. Aston Bing and Martin Zing were famous for singing romantic ballads under water and juggling small dogs. Their act was popular among British motoring engineers before World War I.

- The Ferrari California takes its name from the California Café in the Italian village of Giani, where durability engineers from Maranello stopped for lunch each day.

- Ford's 5-litre 'Coyote' V8 engine derives some of its impressive 307kW output from a ninth cylinder, located under the sump.

- Lord Stanley Oversteer, a gentleman racer from Knightsbridge, invented the technique of hanging out the tail. His first performance of the feat was at the Brooklands circuit in 1929 in the chain-driven aero-engined special known as Flippy Floppy Pip Pop. The manoeuvre lasted fewer than five seconds, by which point the row of three nine-cylinder radial engines had shredded the rear tyres, rims and spokes down to the axles. Years were spent developing 'the Lord Stanley'. It was only after World War II that it was commonly called 'the Oversteer'. An obituary is published on page 310.

12 The reticence of the Swiss

Why don't those cheese-puncturing central Europeans build a decent car?

They already make cogs, gears and spindles for watches with, well, Swiss precision. So why don't they just upsize their engineering a bit?

It would be easy to be cynical and say because they are too busy making Toblerone, financing wars and managing the bank accounts of despots and corporate criminals. Very, very easy. But let's move on.

Casting over the expanses of the Swiss car industry immediately brought to mind only three brands. The first is Monteverdi, which built a few US-engined sports coupes in the 1960s and 1970s.

An early 1970s Monteverdi.

Another is Sbarro. Its scant fame comes from it building a car that scared small children at the 2010 Geneva motor show. Called the Autobau, it looked like a cross between a food blender and a really ugly food blender.

Creating the world's Most Hideous and Altogether Daft Car is no mean feat, because the only other Swiss company that comes to mind – Rinspeed – is constantly vying for the title.

Rinspeed turns out a concept car each year or so, with a new gimmick (amphibiousness, for example) and styling the horror of which probably can't be adequately described in any of Switzerland's four official languages.

So am I underestimating the country's car industry? According to the Swiss Car Register, about seventy-five companies of that hilly land have built motorised vehicles since 1800-and-something.

They include the Egg, the Pic-Pic, the Zebra and the Popp. No, I can't think why they wouldn't have succeeded. The most frightening thing I learned is that the makers of that ghastly Sbarro Autobau run the

The reborn Weber
from 2007.

'sole school for automobile design in Switzerland'. J-e-s-s-u-s!

The Register tells us that the Weber, built from 1899 to 1906, was a passenger car with 'variable wheel diameter'. So much for Swiss precision.

The Weber brand name was revived in 2007 for a Swiss supercar. It looks like it was styled by someone who attended the Sbarro Institute of Design, but still failed all their courses.

There are at least two other Swiss 'supercar' makers. One is Leblanc, a company that must have built upwards of a handful of cars. The other is Orca. This may or may not have ceased production, so fine is the line between going the way they were going, and stopping.

As alluded to before, Switzerland does export things with wheels. They are watches, though at least some of them are branded with car names. The Breitling for Bentley is one example; Porsche Design another.

Mechanical watches are sold on the idea that you are taking part in an ownership experience rather than, for instance, receiving the most accurate timing. That's available for free on your phone or computer.

One thing is pretty obvious if you flick through luxury magazines, or watch Formula One or yachting (just joking – nobody watches yachting, not even the people involved). At least 90 per cent of the purchase price of one of these ludicrously costly time-approximators must disappear into the marketing budget.

Jaeger-LeCoultre, Tag Heuer et al. keep alive the world's glossiest publications, their double-page ads attempting to prove that one impossibly expensive and bejewelled lump of ostentation is better than another.

The Orca.

While flicking through one such mag I discovered a Swiss company called Rado has developed a 'breakthrough'. It's a digital watch (with a display just like a $9.95 Casio) but one powered by a mechanical movement. Yours for just under $4000.

So there you have it. If Switzerland's industrial scions are hell-bent on proving that there is something less relevant than a mechanical watch, namely a digital mechanical watch, any attempt at a family car will have a steam engine, a crank start and a million-dollar price tag. But think of the ownership experience.

13 Let's look at the research

One of the great satisfactions in academia must be to spend several long hard years researching a subject, then see it reduced to a few hundred flippant words by a harried journalist on deadline. And who are we to deny such pleasures to that learned breed?

First a trope or two. Writing about research often involves an implication that the journalist alone unearthed the information while reviewing the original and almost impenetrable 50,000-word report, rather than, say, found the university press release in his or her inbox or stumbled onto the BBC 'Science Report' where some learned Brit on wages really did struggle through every word of the original and almost impenetrable 50,000 word report.

This writer of course is above such cheap tricks. He's too busy working his way through the papers from a recent British Psychological Society's annual conference. It was there, incidentally, that he noticed an intriguing study about babies and cars.

Researchers found that from the moment they first crawl, boys show more interest in toy cars, while girls prefer toy people (otherwise known as dolls).

The study involved ninety children aged from nine to thirty-six months and showed a consistent intrinsic bias towards 'gender-typical' toy choices in babies. Researcher Sara Amalie O'Toole Thommessen said: 'It was very obvious that even the youngest children went straight for gender-typed toys and colours. Boys went straight for the ball and the black car, and girls went to the teddy bear and the doll.'

Another researcher added that they were surprised to find the differences so early. Where were they working – the Institute of the Bleeding Obvious? No, it seems. They were conducting their studies at City University in London.

There are parents, particularly of boys, that don't allow 'gender-typical' toys in their houses. They are what are known as first-time parents. As we all know, by the time the second boy comes along, the house is littered with plastic representations of machine guns, long swords, drag cars, war-hammers, chainsaws, guillotines, Hummers and tactical nuclear weapons.

But I digress. Another recent piece of motoring research (recent, as in 'since the French Revolution'; that's another science journalism trick) involved examining fifty-three potentially angering driving-related

situations and yielding a thirty three-item driving anger scale (with six reliable subscales involving hostile gestures, illegal driving, police presence, slow driving, discourtesy and traffic obstructions).

This work by Deffenbacher, Oetting, Lynch and Rebekah (published in the American Psychological Association's PsycINFO database) showed men were more angered by police presence and slow driving; for women it was illegal behaviour and traffic obstructions. I'm not sure if you've been keeping up with the *Journal of Applied Social Psychology*. It's not as dry a read as you might expect; there's a terrific crossword for a start. Anyway, according to the article 'Territorial Markings as a Predictor of Driver Aggression and Road Rage', drivers with personalised number plates, stickers, decals and other 'territorial markers' are more aggressive than other drivers.

The statement is true even if their stickers and/or decals are calling for peace, love and understanding, according the report's authors, William Szlemko et al.

'The more markers a car has, the more aggressively the person tends to drive when provoked,' Szlemko told the *Washington Post* (though not until after this writer had ploughed through every word of his original research).

It's apparently all about 'owning the road'. People who cover their car with markers see the streets they drive down as private property and other users as intruders. They are far more likely to use their vehicles to express rage when others invade their personal space. So if you see a clever bumper sticker, read it quickly then get out of the way.

Anyway, that's what the research tells us. And now it's been in print here as well. So it's doubly true.

MOTORING CULTURE

14 Ode to Monaro: a lost literary classic

It was published in 1973, the same year Patrick White gave us *The Eye of the Storm*.

White would go on to win the Nobel Prize, while Henry Williams and his defining work, *My Love Had a Black Speed Stripe*, quickly slipped from public consciousness.

So perhaps we can explain a bit about Williams's unique book and let you decide whether such a vast imbalance is fair.

To write an entire novel as an ode to the Holden Monaro is an audacious literary feat – and one that Patrick White certainly wasn't game to attempt. Yet Henry Williams begins confidently: 'Love me, love my Holden. I laid that on the line with the missus before we were spliced.'

The main character, Ron, lives in Blue Gum Drive with Rose. He hocks himself to buy the car of his dreams. Fortunately he works on the GM-H line and can get a discount on a V8 manual (no engine size is mentioned). Not just that, but a word with Oscar the Greek in the paint shop ensures Ron's car receives four coats instead of three. In the end she's 'a blue that never was on land or sea; she was like something out of this world'. Ron is a bit of a philosopher. Although love at first sight

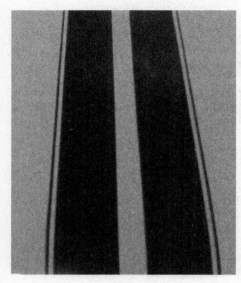

is possible with a woman, he muses, it never lasts. But with a Monaro …

He believes it's no coincidence that the world was created in six days, as that's also how long his car took, from the first spot weld in the body shop to the fitting of the chrome badges at the end: 'I sometimes think if this world had been put together with the same care and precision and workmanship that went into my Monaro it would be in better shape …'

So far so good, but Ron's loving attention to his prized machine plays badly in Blue Gum Drive. He is soon beset with 'missus trouble' and chooses to sleep in the garage instead.

The dust jacket claims Henry Williams once worked on the Holden line, though doesn't say whether this was purely for literary research, like George Orwell going down the coal mine. Either way, there are interesting details about the Holden production process of the early 1970s.

PC this book is not. Ron reckons sheilas shouldn't be allowed to drive V8s because they're not up to it. When they talk about anything serious he wishes they'd 'stay on their own pitch, yakking about curtains and fashions and the price of soap and the clothes other sheilas are wearing'. He isn't keen on migrants or pointy-heads either. The next-door neighbour, Michael, is both. Ron laments the folly of bringing in people who use big words and can't even identify a 5/8 ring spanner.

Rose, losing the battle for Ron's affection, turns vandal. The sight of his damaged Monaro sends Ron into a rage that – *spoiler alert* (no, not that sort of spoiler) – forces him to destroy the thing he most loves. *And* the nagging sheila.

Through deft planning, he manages to load up the Monaro with Rose, the sneering next-door neighbours and, as a special never-to-be-repeated bonus, his annoying foreman.

Having secretly doctored the brakes and steering, Ron's feelings are exceedingly mixed as he stands and watches his Monaro 'moving off like some proud doomed galleon ... setting off on her last journey'. There are no survivors and Ron's guilt seems to be restricted to the Monaro, now 'a tangled heap of junk at the bottom of Alligator Creek.' At the book's conclusion he buys a standard Kingswood because 'love, the real thing, the thing that stops the clock' happens only once in any bloke's lifetime. He's had his Monaro and must move on.

Surely, compared with all that, *The Eye of the Storm* is just a load of purple prose about a batty old woman.

15 Why do racers talk in clichés?

Mr Megastar, thanks for joining us. Perhaps you could tell us why the average motor-racing driver answers almost every question from a selection of about twelve stock expressions.

The boys did a great job.

Sorry?

The boys did a great job. It's a credit to the team. They gave me a terrific car.

But you didn't finish the first lap. You were classified last.

Look, I think you'll find there's a lot more to come from this package. We're here to win races.

That's something else I want to ask about … the use of the majestic plural.

Well, it's quite simple. We got out there in the practice sessions and found our rhythm and stayed out of trouble. We didn't make any mistakes and we were rewarded with some very impressive lap times.

We? Was there someone else in the car?

As I said, we were the people to beat early on, and we took the performance to a new level.

Could it be just false modesty: you shy away from saying 'I'm bloody good,' in favour of 'We're a bloody good team,' even though you egocentric creatures believe it's you that wins and the team that loses?

It might have looked easy out there, but we were battling at every point. We worked on our strategy. We stuck to our guns.

That doesn't really address the issue, does it?

The guys back at the factory too. Working late every night. They've got every right to be proud of themselves.

But the gearbox exploded within 50 metres of the start, showering the first three rows of the Pit Row grandstand with hot metal.

Sure, it wasn't the result we were looking for. But there's a lot we can take away from today.

Yes, but it's spread out fairly widely and may have some sharp edges. Is there a chance of the car staying together next time?

It's been a learning experience. We have a long road ahead of us to close the gap. But as always, we'll be giving it 110 per cent, driving the wheels off.

Is that wise? Wouldn't it be better to keep them on?

Obviously we've done our homework. There's a long way to go. It could be anyone's championship. It's all going to come down to tyres.

Not if you've driven the wheels off. Can we talk about your disqualification for rampant cheating?

Look, I'm not going to comment on these baseless …

… Twice proven in a court of law …

… allegations. We can bounce back from here even stronger.

And also your recent arrest inside that club, allegedly specialising in under-age sadomasochists?

This is a dangerous business we are involved in, and you have to give it respect. The result could have been a lot worse, all things considered. It's not the end of our season.

Are you avoiding that question for fear of upsetting sponsors?

I'm glad you've mentioned them, because it's great to have so much support from SponsorOne, SponsorTwo and SponsorThree.

But they've all announced they are leaving. Didn't you read today's paper?

Look, the boys did a great job and this one is for them – a real team effort.

You're not listening to the questions at all, are you?

Well, that's motor racing.

MEN AND MACHINES
16 What strong men drive

Hitler may have dreamed up the VW Beetle, but he chose to be driven around in massive Benzes.

Lenin was a Rolls-Royce man, but after World War II Stalin ordered a gargantuan ZIS 110, a Russian rip-off of a Packard 180 sedan.

Argentinian despot Juan Perón (and his dodgy wife Eva, aka Evita) showed a bent for Cadillacs and Packards. In the Mao era, China's elite prowled around in massive Red Flag limousines.

Lenin's half-track Rolls-Royce Silver Ghost.

When he wasn't busy garnering 130 per cent of the popular vote, President Marcos of the Philippines was conveyed in a Mercedes-Benz 600 Pullman, as was Yugoslavia's Tito and Romania's Ceaușescu (though Ceaușescu also had a 1974 Buick Electra). Spain's Generalissimo Franco was a Benz man too, with a six-wheeled G4.

Even if one disregards cruel comments about phallic objects, there is clearly a connection between big and flash cars and leaders who won't brook dissent.

Religious and spiritual leaders don't mind a showy set of wheels either. Before the introduction of the fishtank-like modern Popemobile, His Holiness was conveyed in presidential-style limousines built by Mercedes and Ford (the latter being the massive Lincoln-based Lehmann-Peterson).

Remember the Bhagwan Shree Rajneesh, the Indian mystic who convinced thousands of Westerners to dress in orange and liberate themselves from monogamy and other silly vestiges of their repressive upbringings?

The Bhagwan wasn't quite a head of state, though he presided over a largely self-contained 'city' in Oregon. Before he was arrested and exported from the USA in 1985, he had acquired more than ninety Rolls-Royces, mainly Silver Spirits and Silver Spurs. These he used only for short drives, usually around his compound so he could be waved at by his devoted followers.

Why so many Rollers? Bhagwan didn't like to use the same one twice, according to the book *Breaking the Spell* by Australian Jane Stork. 'When he owned a car in every colour and combination made, he had a paint shop built in his garage and had new cars painted in

Kim Jong-il's
official portrait.

unique colours and designs before he ever drove them. Only he drove
them, and then only to go for his daily drive.'

Stork adds that Bhagwan was such a terrible driver that a back-up
vehicle followed discretely behind 'to pull him out of ditches'.

North Korea's Kim Jong-il (1941–2011) had a weakness for Benzes
and, less obviously, Nissans. More bizarrely, at one point he had his top
echelons carted around in local copies of the SsangYong Chairman.

Why anyone would copy the SsangYong Chairman is hard to divine.
It's a little like being a Billy Joel impersonator. It doesn't matter how
much work you put into it, or how well you do it, the best you can ever
be is as good as Billy Joel.

It seems the 'Dear Leader' (one of his official titles, along with
Supreme Commander of the Korean People's Army) had something of
a love-hate relationship with cars. Which is to say he generally loved
having them, and hated it when other people did.

Perhaps that's what drove Kim to issue a 2007 order that all Japanese cars were to be confiscated. One story suggested this happened after the World's Oldest Pre-schooler (OK, that one's not an official title) visited the grave of his late, deified father. On the way home his motorcade – which was typically made up of ten identical cars to confuse would-be assassins – was blocked by a wrecked Japanese car.

Why were there even Japanese cars in North Korea? Most were brought in second-hand through China, following the failure of the few Volga and other Soviet-bloc cars that had been the previous mainstay of the car-driving elite.

The ultimate status symbol during Kim Jong-il's reign was a European car with number plates beginning with the number 216. That told everyone the car was a gift from the man with the Mandate of Heaven. The numbers marked the date of Kim's birthday, February 16. And what a birthday it was. Official biographies suggest that the Dear Leader's arrival in the world was heralded by the appearance of a double rainbow over Mount Baekdu, a new star in the heavens, birds singing in human voices and more. Some North Koreans sincerely believe this. Then again, some Westerners believe, 'I am currently out of the office with no access to email.'

17 The worst Holdens ... ever

In the interests of healthy debate, here's a list of Holden horrors, ranging from the inarguable to the fisticuffable. Your squabbling time starts now.

Barina Cabrio – There have been some pretty marginal Barinas through the years. However, the locally adapted Cabrio of 1997 – claimed as the company's first convertible passenger car – wasn't marginal at all. It was unambiguously atrocious. It twisted, you shouted. And it leaked like a sieve made by Lancia.

Piazza – This Isuzu-sourced aberration was old when it arrived here (in 1986), yet bad even when it was new. This 'sports coupe' was also ridiculously expensive. As for roadholding, if you ran a handling *comparo* between it and a bag of shit, it is quite possible the bag of shit would win. Other than that, nothing much to report. A couple of young guys drove one all the way around Australia a few years ago and wrote a book about it. Everest had already been climbed.

EK – The FB was a belated homage to the '57 Chevrolet (which came out in 1956; Yanks were never good at getting year models right). The ever-so-mildly updated EK version maintained the same comprehensive catalogue of trends that had receded: sharp tail-fins, dogleg windscreen pillars, dome roof and so on. And it was still on sale in 1962, by which time the Falcon made it look like an ancient curio.

LH Torana: problems staying together from the start.

Torana LH – Yes, it won Bathurst, but that was in modified form. As a road car, the 1974 Torana was heavy, thirsty, expensive, cramped and looked like a Gemini suffering from water retention.

HD – An unfortunate interlude between the EH and HR, both world class. It had avant-garde styling, in the sense that its avant guards stuck right out, threatening any pedestrians.

Scurry – A micro-van with Dumbo-inspired styling, which was clearly a Suzuki in every way except for the badges that said Holden. If anyone actually bought a Scurry, that person kept it very quiet (perhaps by putting the original badges back on).

Brougham – This 'luxury flagship' (yeah, right) lasted from 1968 until 1971, through HK, HT and HG versions. Instead of a long wheelbase to match the new Fairlane, it had a long and highly decorated arse. Presumably to fight off carnivores.

VL Group A – For about two-and-a-half times the price of a standard Commodore, 'The Walkinshaw' of 1988 brought fuel-injection and a useful tweak or two. But why damn it with faint praise when there's good solid abuse? It was the most unspeakably ugly thing on the road. People pre-ordered them in the hope they would appreciate. For the first decade or two the price fell down a mineshaft.

Scurry. Quick, or you'll have to drive it.

Nova – To anyone else it was a 1989 Corolla. So why not buy the original?

Apollo – See Nova. This one was an uninspiring Camry (sorry, is there another type?), with afterthought Holden badges. The only thing as silly was the Commodore-based Lexcen with afterthought Toyota badges.

Camira JB – You know, the 1.6-litre from 1982. If cars went to school, this one would be in the giftless and untalented class. Curiously, it sold only to people who were otherwise going to buy a Commodore, giving Holden the joy of building two completely separate models for exactly the same sales total.

Commodore VP – Didn't matter what was in the range, as soon as they put rear wheel spats onto the Calais variant, the VP became a legitimate target for ridicule and derision. It looked like it was purpose-built for eighty-year-old Miamians.

Viva – It was one of a group of rebadged Daewoos that made it here circa 2005 and were as bad as each other. With the Viva (as in *viva la lack of difference*), Holden couldn't find a price point low enough to convince Australians they should do anything but run away.

18 Who talks the most twaddle?

That's a tough one. In the automotive world, there's business twaddle, marketing twaddle, legal twaddle and much more beside.

But let's start with styling. After all, car designers are such experts at talking complete and utter bollocks. They use what is known as 'design language' in their work and, when it is translated into English, it isn't very stylish.

Take Hyundai and 'Fluidic sculpture,' which is a 'new design philosophy which embodies a flowing and dynamic form execution. Hyundai Design embraces the harmony of human co-existence and the wisdom of sustainable growth from nature's never ending evolution to create a vision of progressive and passionate future design'. Top-notch poppycock, sure, though to be fair it's been filtered through a marketing team. So what about when designers are allowed to speak for themselves?

Here's Jason Castriota on the (now deceased) Saab PhoeniX: 'We call it "aeromotional" … We wanted to communicate a connection between the outside and the inside of the car and this large, translucent ice block, housing our passengers and the mechanicals, helps us to do it by creating visual depth and interest.'

One day scholars will find a Stylist's Rosetta Stone and work out what the hell he was on about.

Saab's Phoenix failed to rise again.

The current Toyota logo was introduced in 1989 with a festival of claptrap: 'The two perpendicular ovals inside the larger oval represent the heart of the customer and the heart of the company … The overlapping of the two perpendicular ovals inside the outer oval symbolize "T" for Toyota, as well as a steering wheel, representing the vehicle itself.

'The outer oval symbolizes the world embracing Toyota … the space in the background within the logo exhibits the "infinite values" which Toyota conveys to its customers.' And so on and so on. Apparently the Hyundai badge represents the company shaking hands with a customer. Rather than, say, some advertising git shaking hands with himself.

Business twaddle is often deliberate doublespeak: reminding shareholders how effectively and efficiently your company is gouging customers, while being sure not to undermine the advertising that proclaims your participation in business is solely to make lasting friendships.

Which is why Woolworths – insert your own abusive descriptive subclause here – talks about terrific 'margin outcomes' in its petrol division. Yep, the punters should miss that.

Chinese carmaker Chery has announced plans to 'progressively increase the ratio of procurement, R&D and talent indigenization to "go out" and take root abroad'. Why not? The company has already 'transited overseas development modes from product export initially to rooted development now, and preliminarily accomplished overseas strategic transformation'. Now, you may think making fun of Chery is unfair because of language differences. However, English-as-a-first-language business publications often write just as much dross.

Twaddle of the legal variety was seen when Ford served Ferrari with a writ for using the term 'F150' for its Formula One race-car. 'Ferrari has misappropriated the F-150 trademark,' it said, 'in order to capitalise on and profit from the substantial goodwill that Ford has developed in the F-150 trademark.'

There are several words that stand out here, including 'goodwill'.

Now if Ferrari named a lithe, attractive, responsive vehicle the F150, and you were making an ugly tank for inbreds that shared the same name, you'd probably accept that if goodwill was on the move, most of it would be coming in your direction.

But, no, Ford's statement suggests it's a bait-and-switch. Yep, we can just imagine some Hicksville Southerner turning up at the local Shotgun-and-Pick-Up Showroom to grab another 3-tonne bungalow on wheels, and tragically ending up with a Ferrari race-car instead.

'You done bought what, Jimmy-Bob? How y'all gunna get your big fat ass in that?'

19 Reviving old brands

Without a doubt, old brands can be revived.

Look at Bugatti. It's gone from being a worm-eaten cadaver to one of the world's great supercar brands, builders of the 400-km/h-plus Veyron.

Then again, look at Bugatti. It's gone from being nobody's problem to a huge financial sinkhole, swallowing hundreds of millions since the first modern attempt to revive it in 1987.

Bugatti Galibier concept.

Under VW's stewardship (since 2000) the resuscitated company has sold a few hundred cars at astronomical prices. But even these prices are not nearly astronomical enough to realise a profit, at current production rates, until ten minutes before hell freezes over.

If relaunching Bugatti has proven anything, it's just how deep your pockets need to be to make such a project work. And frankly, VW still hasn't proven that it can make Bugatti work.

Look at the long, long fight to revive Saab, which involved Holland's Spyker, a venerable automotive brand with a heritage going back to the start of the twentieth century.

Any brand with a history that long should have known something about this difficult business, shouldn't it? Well, yes, but there was a small gap in the Spyker timeline. It faded out completely between the mid-1920s and the year 2000.

Spyker, of course, wasn't really Spyker. It was yet another case of an old badge being dug up and zapped with a defibrillator, on behalf of yet another new company with dreams of turning out world-beating sports cars.

Spyker promised to preserve the 'Swedishness of the Saab brand', no doubt while affirming the Dutchness of its own sports cars. The original Spyker slogan was *Nulla tenaci invia est via*,

Spyker's Peking-to-Paris model (yes, it really is called that).

which, considering it all ended in tears, was probably Latin for 'good luck, boyo'.

There is almost no automotive badge that someone doesn't dream of resuscitating. We're told Trabant, Frazer-Nash and Detroit Electric will soon be among the undead. Pierce-Arrow cars are supposedly available out of Switzerland (one reborn model looks like a Batmobile, though is less restrained).

Packard was put up for sale in 2008. About US$1.5 million bought the right to revive the brand name of the late Packard car company (1899–1958) and to manufacture the modern-day Twelve limousine. The only potential problems were (a) few people remember Packards as anything other than 1950s barges and (b) the modern-day Twelve limousine.

Not quite sure who designed the Twelve – perhaps nobody – but this '21st-century rendition of a Packard ultra-luxury automobile' looks uglier than the world's ugliest person pulling an ugly face. The bulging flanks are supposed to recall pre-war elegance, but bring to mind post-war flab. And the grille … quick, somebody, dial Triple Zero.

The reborn Packard. Going cheap.

Alvis hasn't quite left the building. New owners are planning to revive production. Curiously, they are starting with the 4.3-litre short chassis tourer, last built in 1937.

This means that, in about three-quarters of a century, the reborn Alvis will make cars that look like today's. It might be too late.

Riley and Triumph were brands that BMW held on to when it ditched the assorted shrapnel that came with Rover Group. Either could one day be inflicted upon us again. Austin-Healey, too. A deal has been signed that may see cars with that badge coming out of the Chinese MG factory.

Jensen has bounced back several times but it seems the coroner is at last reporting no further movement. Allard has yelled out 'I'm not dead yet' a couple of times, too, as has AC Cars. AC now seems to be based in Germany (via the US and Malta) and is building, you guessed it, Cobras.

Fortunately, Armstrong-Siddeley, Bond, Clyno, Panther, Crossley and Jowett aren't building anything. If they start, I think it's up to all of us to make them stop.

Former Fiat exec Gian Mario Rossignolo, who tried to revive legendary Italian marque Isotta-Fraschini in the 1990s, is down in the cellar with Igor running electricity though the body of another deceased Italian.

This time it's De Tomaso, the brand associated with the stylish but slapdash Pantera and Mangusta coupés of the 1960s and 1970s. These were Italian-built, American Iron-powered semi-classics. Amazingly, Rossignolo now reckons he can build eight thousand new De Tomasos a year. Yes, eight thousand. A year. As they say at Spyker: *Nulla tenaci invia est via.*

20 Which car should Dave buy?

The dilemma

Dave wants a roomy, practical family car that is safe and environmentally efficient. He is not an enthusiastic driver but appreciates high retained value and low service costs. He works in the retail industry and occasionally needs to transport small appliances from shop to shop, so a wagon might be useful. The budget is $35,000. His wife, Felicity, insists on climate-control air-conditioning and prefers cloth seats. She has been unfaithful to Dave for much of the past decade. She has also been secretly diverting money from their joint bank account to prop up her brother's IT business. Dave doesn't much like his two children, Harrison, nineteen, and Montego, thirteen, either.

Our advice

There are several cars that will adequately fill your brief, Dave. The Camry, the Mazda 6, the Suzuki Kizashi. All are well built and solid, with good efficiency. There's also that overly styled Hyundai thing which looks like a Mercedes CLS gone wrong. No, forget that. You did mention resale. Same for the Holden Cruze.

If you want European (real European, not Korean-built French cars), your budget will be quickly eclipsed. Still, when someone expects so little of life, it's hard to go past the Camry. It's the sensible, safe choice.

But here's the rub: it's not for you, Dave. Comes a time when you have to look the world squarely in the eye and say, 'Enough is enough'.

Do you want engraved on your tombstone: 'He drove a roomy, practical family car with high retained values'?

We're not going to psychoanalyse you (not on a motoring journalist's wage), but you may be using a new car as a defence mechanism. You may be thinking the consistency and outward stability implied by a solid, dependable, practical car – in white, no doubt – will divert attention from Harrison's increasing drug use and, lately, his tentative forays into dealing.

Or Montego's stupid name. Or your own deepening conviction that they are never going to leave home. Not until they've bled you dry.

A roomy, practical family car will encourage Montego to demand you ferry her and her friends around. Though you'll still have to drop them 200 metres from where they're going. Harrison will borrow it to do his collections.

Worse still, no new car, no matter how conservative, will stop the neighbours talking about the squalid goings-on at number 43. Nor will it encourage the wife to change her wayward ways. Look at your grim, turgid life, Dave. It's hard to blame the neighbours. And it's hard to blame Felicity.

By the way, it's Montego's soccer coach now. Your wife's ditched the maths teacher. Sorry to be the one to bring the news.

Anyway, our recommendation is the Porsche 911 Carrera S. Yes, it's expensive, Dave, but less so than, say, a Ferrari 250 GTO. And the real cost of even a Carrera S is far less than a wasted life.

Think of the statistics: 294 kW and 440 Nm. Seven-speed PDK transmission. Rest to 100 km/h in 4.3 seconds.

Any appliances you plan to move from shop to shop will need to be small, but you can make several trips if need be. The top speed is 304 km/h, for chrissakes.

Admittedly your budget will cover only the first few lease payments. So mortgage the house. Then torch it and drive over the soccer coach and into the sunset, flat out in first, second, third, fourth, fifth …

A fig for the Camry and its like, Dave. Another fig for the kids, the wife, and working in retail. For one brief shining moment you need to live. Really live.

Disclaimer: This advice is advisory only. Derr. Potential car-buyers should make independent inquiries and reach decisions based on their own circumstances, whether their spouse is having it off with a sporting instructor, and whether provocation is a valid excuse for grievous bodily harm and arson in their state or territory.

21 Unbearable lightness

An edition of the official Lotus magazine quoted company founder Colin Chapman saying – sardonically, one hopes – that 'Any car that holds together for a whole race is too heavy.'

The same man uttered: 'You'd never catch me driving a Lotus race-car.'

A Lotus official nervously explained that Chapman didn't mean that his cars were so light and frail as to be dangerous, as many interpreted it. Chapman meant they were so quick that, if he were driving one, *you'd never catch me*.

In both cases, let's give the man the benefit of the doubt because his basic philosophy – 'simplify, then add lightness' – is music to any sports-car lover's ears.

Lotus ingenuity in that department went a long way – occasionally too far. The original Europa of 1966 had fixed side windows because winding or sliding mechanisms would add cost, complexity and increase the all-up weight of 610 kilograms.

Who needs air, anyway?

Despite Chapman's mantra, and despite incontrovertible proof that a light car can deliver smile-inducing performance even with a modestly powered engine, cars have been larding up ever since the 1960s. Despite all the new technology we've brought to bear.

Lightness in motion: Lotus Elise Club Racer.

Part of the problem is that sports-car drivers have turned into a bunch of precious princesses. The Europa had seats that were fixed too. If they didn't suit, you simply crawled down the coffin-like foot-well, head first with a torch and spanner, and adjusted the pedals.

The 2012 Lotus Elise Club Racer had sliding seats but, otherwise, did without decent weather protection, seat padding or soundproofing in order to deliver an all-up weight of 852 kilograms.

Did the average buyer want such austerity? No, siree. They were far more likely to specify the soft trim, sound system and air-con, undoing much of the good work. Today's sports-car drivers even demand safety features, further proving how soft they've become.

Look at some of the things we're calling sports cars: the Bentley Continental GT coupe, which weighs nearly 2.4 tonnes. Even the 4WD – the McMansion of the Macadam – has somehow acquired the moniker Sport Utility Vehicle.

In its most extreme form, the Hummer H1 'SUV' was nearly 3.5 tonnes. Some sport.

Porsche once called a car the '550' after its weight in kilograms. Its bestselling product is now the Cayenne, which is nearly four times as porculent. Admittedly, it was once easier to be light because you could simply build something grossly unsafe. That's how the Zeta Sports – an oxymoron if ever there was one – could lightly dust the scales at 400 kilograms.

The modern Bugatti Veyron – the point at which all weird car statistics converge – certainly boasts sports-car acceleration and cornering. But, at nearly 1,900 kilograms, it requires 736 kW to achieve its 400 km/h-plus top speed.

Stick its 8-litre W16 engine in, say, a new generation Morgan three-wheeler and then we'd all be reminded of the days when driving a sports car meant you were brave, skilled and completely insensitive to weather or having the end of your spine centre-punched at every bump.

The one place great weight isn't a problem – or a sign of princess-ness – is at very high speed in a straight line. It can keep you on the ground, which is always handy.

The supersonic Thrust SSC weighed 10 tonnes. The same team's Bloodhound, chasing 1,600 km/h, will be a comparatively lithe 7 tonnes despite having onboard an E200 jet, a Falcon rocket and a Cosworth F1 engine.

I'd call that sports. Just maybe not car.

No power to the people: Zeta Sports.

22 What's the top Toyota?

You might say 'the Lexus,' in which case you'd be both rude and wrong. It's actually the Toyota Century Royal, a monumental limousine built for the Japanese Imperial Household.

Stretching more than 6 metres, weighing about 3 tonnes and powered by a 5-litre V12, it dwarfs any other car coming out of Toyota City. Well, it would do, if it came out of Toyota City, but apparently it's built under contract by the Kanto Auto Works subsidiary in Shizuoka.

Toyota itself isn't perhaps set up for runs of less than a kazillion, and the Century Royal production total stands at approximately four.

The Century Royal dwarfs other Toyotas and most other sedans. Motorcade footage makes it look like a normal car that, due to a computer glitch, has been built on a different scale to everything else. Its bonnet and boot plateaus about halfway up everyone else's windscreens.

Features include suicide doors at the rear and granite steps so that the royal feet can step in and out on a solid bit of igneous rock rather than vulgar man-made surfaces. The head lining is rice paper with inset lights to give the appearance, or at least ambience, of a Japanese stateroom.

The Toyota Century Royal was presented to the Emperor in 2006, replacing some rather ancient Nissan Prince Royals used up until then.

The Royal Century.

Although a very limited edition, the imperial jalopy is based on the standard Century, which remains the top car from Toyota, hard to fathom though that might be.

The Century was first seen in 1967 and, when it received its one and only update (thus far) thirty years later, it was cleverly restyled to look almost exactly the same.

The original had a 3-litre V8 and was shaped a bit like a Russian copy of a 1964 Lincoln. The slightly smoother bodywork of 1997 cloaked four extra cylinders and a couple of extra litres.

In Maslow's Hierarchy of Cars, even the standard Century sits above any Lexus, though only in the Japanese domestic market where everything is just a little curious.

Despite an unlimited colour choice, most Centurys are painted black, with doilies on the seats, white lace curtains, and a gloved-and-capped driver doing the honours for some aged bizzoid or government hack in the back.

By some reports, the Century is also favoured by the Yakuza criminal groups. That makes sense, as they work closely with the government at times.

The Century is priced above the Lexus line-up, with the rather idiosyncratic marketing line that it is the sort of product 'acquired by long hard work in a plain but formal suit'. Most publicity seems to be about quietness, and the whole rear-drive package rides on air suspension that gives 'a calmness of a type unequalled in the world'. A rare English language promotional video says: 'The essence of the Century's hospitality is epitomised by the rear seats.' These leaning, tilting, massaging rear pews are linked to the doors. When they are opened (automatically, of course), the seats return to their standard position for easy ingress and egress.

Oddly, there's a trapdoor in the front passenger seat so the bigwig in the back can stretch his legs even further.

Toyota sells only a few hundred Centuries a year (600 by one report) but the V12 is available in no other model. Weird or what?

And if one car in this odd micro-niche is not enough, Nissan also made the V8-powered President from the mid-1960s, while Mitsubishi produced the Debonair, which looked like a Chinese knock-off of a Russian copy of a 1964 Lincoln.

The Nissan died of natural causes in 2012. The Debonair went front-wheel drive with semi-contemporary styling in the 1980s, then was marched behind the shed and put out of everyone else's misery in 1999. The Century alone survives.

23 The art of taking it with you

Whether you can really 'take it with you when you go' may depend on your belief system, but some people have tried. Californian oil heiress Sandra Ilene West specified in her will that she be buried 'in my lace nightgown … in my Ferrari, with the seat slanted comfortably'. Her wish was granted perhaps earlier than she planned, as West died at the age of just thirty-seven.

A Crazy Coffins Gullwing Mercedes funeral urn, with 410.5 cubic inches (for the ashes).

The year was 1977 and *Time* magazine reported: 'Like Egypt's King Tutankhamen, who had a couple of golden chariots buried near him when he died in 1352 BC, [West] is journeying to the hereafter in style.'

Time reported that West's Ferrari was a powder-blue 1964 330 America. Most other reports said West specified that it should be her favourite Ferrari, a far more valuable Ferrari 250GT.

Proof of which car is really down there might be hard to, *ahem*, dig up. Although a large crowd and TV cameras attended, the casket-on-wheels was packed inside a huge grey crate. After the crate was craned into the rather large open plot, it was covered with a hefty slab of cement to deter any particularly determined and ghoulish car thieves.

The plain gravesite, at the San Antonio cemetery in Texas, gives no clue to the extent of what's below. West, however, is not the only person to request their hearse doesn't stop next to the grave.

Most of us wouldn't be seen dead in a 1973 Pontiac Catalina, but Lonnie Holloway had no such inhibitions. In 2009 the ninety-year-old North Carolinian went subterranean in his monstrous yank tank with his hunting rifles in the boot and a hundred-dollar note in his top pocket.

Eleven years earlier one Rose Martin, eighty-four, of Rhode Island, had taken up four burial plots when she and her white Chevrolet Corvair were deposited six-feet (and four-wheels) under. A Corvair? But aren't they unsafe?

More modest was the automotive send-off for India's Narayan Swami in 2007. He chose to decompose in the Morris Minor he bought new in 1958. Villagers in Sivapuram decorated the car before lowering it and its owner into the earth.

The Ga tribe in Ghana has a thing for brightly coloured fantasy coffins. At least one person has been buried in a small-scale wooden S-Class, another in a large-scale bottle of Coca-Cola. Caskets made to look like mobile phones are popular too.

An English coffin maker, Vic Fearn & Company, is trying to put the *fun* back into *fun*eral with a range of 'Crazy Coffins'. They include guitars, train carriages, boats, skateboards – and cars. One of their most intricate jobs is a wooden 1920s Rolls-Royce Phantom, with room for one.

The Rolls coffin from Vic Fearn & Company Ltd.

Most car buffs leave their favourite machines above ground, though sometimes with a twist. Britain's Steve Marsh had always been obsessed with BMWs. When he died of heart failure his family organised for a unique headstone: a full-size M3 convertible rendered from a single piece of granite.

Weighing a tonne and costing £50,000, including the shipping from China where it was built, the monumental Beamer was unveiled in 2010. The response was mixed, but to hell with the critics – you only die once! Unless you are a Buddhist, of course, in which case you can perhaps simply bequeath your favourite motor to your next incarnation. And hope you don't come back as an insect.

A recent trend – at least among certain groups – is a public viewing in your favourite vehicle. In 2003 Alexander Bernard Harris, a hip-hop mogul from Miami, died of natural causes (for a hip-hop mogul from Miami). He was shot in the head by up to four gunmen while having his hair styled.

Harris's body was displayed at the funeral home sitting behind the wheel of his yellow Lamborghini Murcielago.

Even creepier, a shooting victim in Puerto Rico attended his own wake, propped up on the seat of his Honda 600 motorcycle. The twenty-two year old was said to be riding the bike 'all the way to heaven'.

24 Test your knowledge and amaze your friends (or not)

1. *True or false*: In 2007 more examples of Mitsubishi Australia's 380 family sedan were returned under its 'Bring it back if you're not completely satisfied' policy than were actually sold.

2. *True or false*: When Michigan authorities began work on the Interstate 496, they decided to name it after automotive pioneer Ransom Eli Olds, the man behind Oldsmobile and REO cars. When the route of the R.E. Olds Freeway was finalised, it ran through Ransom's heritage-listed mansion, which was flattened.

3. *True or false*: The F259 Guido Ferrari was named after the nephew of company founder Enzo who, three months earlier, had been christened F259 Guido Ferrari.

4. *True or false*: The Bugatti Veyron is famous for its sixteen-cylinder engine but an engine with even more cylinders was originally contemplated.

5. *True or false*: The original car-making Ford, Henry I, came within 2,200 votes of becoming a US senator.

6. *True or false*: The Lada Samara is built in the Italian city of Togliatti.

7.   *True or false*: World motorcycle champion and, later, motor sport commentator Barry Sheene performed in Puccini's opera *Tosca* at Covent Garden alongside the legendary singers Maria Callas and Tito Gobbi.

8.   *True or false*: SsangYong's Musso model was named after a Romanian word that translates as 'big and ugly but quite strong'.

9.   *True or false*: Dan Gurney's victory in the 1967 Le Mans 24-Hour race was notable not just because it was Ford's second victory in a row (with the GT40) but because it was the first time a winning driver sprayed the champagne rather than merely drinking it.

10. *True or false*: In Land Speed Record breaking, the 600 km/h mark was passed in 1947. Englishman John Cobb used his *Railton Mobil Special* to set this new record of 634.27 km/h, beating his 1939 mark of 595.3 km/h. In 1952 he was killed by the Loch Ness Monster.

NB: Answers are on page 315.

25 How many cars in the average movie?

Seventeen. Yes, seventeen. It seems unlikely, yet there's statistical proof.

Where? We'll come to that shortly.

It started with a search to find out more about the seriously cool cars in the television series *Mad Men*. This search provided an interesting reminder of the Slightly Sad Obsession (SSO) that is such a big part of film/television buff-dom.

Indeed, which is such a big part of the Internet. The web contains heated comments arguing, for example, that a certain model wasn't available until August and, as the episode in question was quite clearly set in April of that year, the directors should be hogtied and beaten.

It's not just arguments about facts. There are issues of character. One posting says *Mad Men* is all wrong. The main character, Don Draper, 'would NEVER have gone from a '60 LeSabre convertible to a '61 Dodge Polara sedan … If Don were upgrading from the '60 LeSabre convertible, he would have stayed in a convertible, almost certainly would have stayed with Buick, or at least GM, and would have gone flashier – maybe a '62 Electra 225 convertible.'

But it's the Internet Movie Cars Database (www.imcdb.org) that contains a whole extra level of SSO. It identifies – as I type – 526,481 cars seen in 30,596 movies, telemovies and television episodes (hence that average of seventeen, or a fraction over).

Hell, it even identifies 305 cars that are found only in deleted scenes. And twenty-seven seen solely in alternative endings.

There are screen grabs of said vehicles too. So if someone is completing important post-doctoral research on, say, 'Depictions of the Holden Monaro in the French Telemovies of Hazanavicius and Mézerette', there's the picture of the 1972 HQ two-door used in their landmark work *Le Grand Détournement*.

The 1966 Bongo van, 1974 AMC Matador and seven other cars used in that same film are also shown. As are shots of Monaros used in everything from 2008's *Two Fists, One Heart*, to *Underbelly, Mad*

Max 2 and that often-overlooked Italian movie from 1971, *Bello, onesto, emigrato Australia sposerebbe compaesana illibata.*

It is not just Monaros – imcdb.org places just as much importance on tracking down movie roles performed by the Daewoo Lacetti (seen in eight films) and the Simca Aronde Commerciale (also seen in eight films). It lists the top brands depicted in films as (in order): Ford, Chevrolet, Mercedes-Benz, VW, Toyota and Renault.

Renault? Yes, the 15,590 hits (compared with 61,710 for Ford) probably has something to do with the huge number of films shot on crowded Paris streets. Australian cars (including the 1968 Valiant Wayfarer ute seen in *The Man from Hong Kong*) score 1,927 hits. That's fifteenth in the table of nations.

And what of *Mad Men,* set in the advertising world of the 1960s? The Internet Movie Cars Database (IMCDb) identifies twenty-five cars from the first series, including an aerial shot in which the outline of a Checker Marathon can be made out. How SSO is that?

There are clearer renditions of such interesting pieces of US iron as a 1959 Oldsmobile Dynamic 88, a 1950 Studebaker Champion Starlight Coupe, a 1957 Hudson Hornet and a 1956 Plymouth Sport Suburban.

The IMCDb is described as

'the result of the cooperative work of several people that like cars and movies, especially when the two are mixed together'. It's a Herculean task that can never be completed or 100 per cent accurate. And think of how many missives they'd get from middle-aged SSO males who live with their mothers, arguing 'that's not the 1971 model, it's the 1971-and-a-half export version with the interim frosted tail-lights'.

In the meantime, the site allows you to categorise film cars according to their roles, for example: 'Vehicle used by a character or in a car chase', and a great deal more. So much for getting any work done.

26 What do they say at car launches?

Gentlemen (and very occasional lady) of the motoring press, it is with great pride that we've brought you here today to introduce our new model, the Obnox ES6.

As you'll see from the photos now up on the screen, it's the model that introduces our new corporate Spatial Apparition Hydro-Dynamic styling.

This distinctive new design direction is something we previewed on our Delusion concept car at this year's Alice Springs Salon de l'Automobile.

It brings together an oversized grille, a questionable crease down each flank and a price rise, and will eventually be extended to all our models. At which point [*sotto voce*] we'll declare it passé and come up with something else.

Shortly, our marketing director will project a series of unintelligible charts showing, among other things, a series of dots randomly sprayed across a rising line. The names of car models will be scattered on either side of this line just as arbitrarily, some matching up with dots, some not.

He will also reveal – can you at the back turn off that freaking phone? – a three-dimensional multi-coloured waterfall chart. It will show where we perceive our positioning, where our competitors perceive our positioning, and where our positioning perceives our customers.

But first a video, showing focus-group vox pops and a camera moving very slowly over early styling sketches. Although these sketches have almost nothing to do with the finished product (which doesn't run on 20 aspect tyres or have letterbox slits for windows), we'll continue to use them, even in the brochures.

Also in this short film, our new head designer breaks new ground in styling-related jargon, and his minions match him phrase for phrase. This is not the only reason for the loud background music, however. Our licensing agent assures us this music is, like the Obnox ES6 itself, very up to date and edgy. Though unfortunately I can't remember the name of the rhythm combo that performed it.

The interior – again shown here by a stylised sketch rather than, say, the real interior – takes on a new aviation theme reflecting our company's rich heritage in that area. Some of you young ones might not be aware that an unrelated division of a company, now owned by the same faceless venture capitalists as us, supplied the seat-frames to Boeing for the 707.

And now I'd like to draw your attention to a screen filled entirely with meaningless numbers. No need to take notes, you in the second row. It's all printed in the press pack and makes just as much sense there.

You'll also find in that press pack some comparative statistics showing how vastly superior our vehicle is in such important areas as rear elbow room, angle of departure and reserve fuel-tank capacity.

Unfortunately, we couldn't fit in power, torque and weight figures, but there are three DVDs full of those styling sketches – and a really snazzy pen with the Obnox logo on it.

Perhaps the best news from a buyer's point of view is that the price rise has been held to just 3 per cent, despite a whole lot of new safety equipment, not absolutely all of which was required by legislation. The warning sticker near the exposed engine fan, for example, was our own initiative.

Just to repeat, despite higher equipment levels the Obnox ES6 is just 3 per cent dearer than the outgoing ES5 [even *sotto voce-ier*], which we hiked by $2,500 last Thursday because we were already out of stock and wanted to lessen the changeover shock.

So, if there are any questions, our team of executives is here to respond to them. Rather than to, say, answer them. But first, I'd like to ask our chairman – fresh from his acquittal and complete exoneration on taxation and price-fixing charges – to officially launch this important new model.

27 Who said what (and why)

'Aerodynamics,' scoffed Enzo Ferrari, 'are for people who can't build engines.'

'I *am* prepared to sell you one of my Aston-Martins at cost,' company owner David Brown told a regular customer who was trying to screw down a special deal, 'but are you really happy to pay so much more than the normal price?'

Ettore Bugatti had a nice line of chat too. He said Bentley made the world's fastest trucks and, when defending the woeful brakes of his own machines, retorted: 'My cars are designed to go, not to stop.'

These lines have been reproduced many times, with wildly varying wording, and are sometimes attributed to car barons other than the ones above.

Likewise, 'You can't make a silk purse out of a pig's ear, but you can make a mighty fast pig.' Carroll Shelby is the popular choice for that one, but who knows, it might have been John DeLorean. Or even Oscar Wilde.

Sir Alec Issigonis is cited by some as originating not only the Morris Minor and Mini-Minor, but the catchcry 'A horse is a camel designed by a committee.' Henry Ford is credited with the most maxims, including one about colours, or lack thereof. The origin of this can be pinned down to a definite date and wording. Sort of.

Ford's autobiography, *My Life and Work*, states: 'In 1909 I announced one morning, without any previous warning, that in the future we were going to build only one model, that the model was going to be "Model T" and that the chassis would be exactly the same for all cars, and I remarked: Any customer can have a car painted any colour that he wants so long as it is black.'

However, Ford's book wasn't published until 1922, and 'in collaboration with Samuel Crowther'. Which is a polite way of saying, it was ghostwritten.

Ford may never have said those actual words; Crowther may have provided them, or perhaps embellished something of Ford's that was similar-ish but less punchy; Ford may have instead invented the quote in 1922, crediting it to his younger self. Or it may have been nicked from Oscar Wilde too.

Henry's name is also attached to numerous variations of: 'Every time I see an Alfa Romeo go by, I tip my hat.' It may have been not a compliment but an acerbic quip; possibly Ford didn't expect an Alfa to make it that far.

Equally, the phrase may have been invented by Alfaholics, as it seems to have first appeared in an Italian book in 1990. By then Henry, like most post-war Alfas, was no longer a going concern.

'What's good for General Motors is good for America,' can be traced to an official record, if not quite in those words.

In 1953 GM boss Charles E. Wilson was offered the position of Secretary of Defense. When asked if this represented a conflict of interest, he told a Congressional Committee: 'What is good for the country is good for General Motors, and vice versa.'

Ernest Hemingway shows a protected species who's boss.

An Ernest Hemingway aphorism is cited endlessly by revheads, hill-climbers and animal-taunters: 'There are only three real sports: auto racing, mountaineering and bullfighting. The rest are games.'

Alas, Hemingway scholars have found no evidence that 'Papa' ever said such a thing. The line was more likely from Barnaby Conrad or Ken Purdy, but they are much less famous men and memorable quotes invariably migrate up the celebrity food chain.

A saying attributed to various car collectors (Pink Floyd's Nick Mason et al.) is, 'If I could get back all the money I've ever spent on cars, I'd spend it on cars.' It's reminiscent of the best known saying of George Best.

The English soccer star – a lively, rarely sober and perhaps not always original after-dinner speaker – slurred out a hundred variations of the delightful: 'I spent 90 per cent of my money on women, drink and fast cars … the rest, I wasted.'

RATTLETRAPS, ETC.
28 The worst Fords ... ever

Well, come on – we have to balance out the Holden list. If we stick only to Fords sold in Australia, herewith is the starting point for pistols at dawn.

Capri Roadster – It might have worked if Mazda – which Ford partly owned – didn't do everything better. The MX-5 was from the heart, the Capri from the parts bin. The styling was questionable, the build quality ghastly, the handling Laser-like and, if the Capri had a soul, that would have leaked too.

Festiva – A little piece of nastiness imported from Kia of South Korea. It was based on the superseded Mazda 121, presumably on a day the photocopier wasn't working properly.

Twenty-fifth Anniversary Falcon GT – You know when the legendary and much-loved band gets back together and they're all bald and one of them has a walking cane, and the singer has been replaced because he died of congestive heart failure a decade earlier? That's what this 1992 effort brought to mind. There were afterthought bits stuck on everywhere, and the stated 200 kW output was nothing if not optimistic.

Landau – This was a lard-nosed version of the Falcon Hardtop with squared-off side openings, and a vinyl roof to hide ugly welds. Sales were slow; so was it. In case anyone mistook this fat, heavy and ponderous machine for a sports car, the American term 'personal coupe' was adopted.

The unloved Capri soft-top.

The droopy Taurus.

Cortina TC – The four-cylinder was merely dull, the six-cylinder was downright spiteful. It combined Falcon economy with Cortina interior space, plus Ford of England fit-and-finish and Olympic-standard understeer. The cabin had a habit of filling with fumes. Look at what the Japanese were doing in the early 1970s and it's obvious why the Cortina wasn't long for this world.

Falcon AU – If the buck-toothed, cross-eyed frontal treatment and droopy tail weren't enough, the build quality was grotesque. Ford quickly put a spoiler on the back and the ute grille on the front to disguise a basic shape that was wronger than wrong. Cleaning up the other glitches took longer.

Laser KH – Can't remember this one, can you? The pudgy, designed-for-America-but-assembled-in-Sydney version of the Laser was forgettable but for its extravagantly inset wheels, apparently to allow chains to be fitted in snowy climes. Great.

Corsair – A rebadged 1986 Nissan Pintara, possibly sold with the logic that if you give a skin disease a different name, it might become desirable. Fortunately, only a few hundred people were fooled.

Falcon EA – As with the later AU, it was a major model change that went badly. Very badly. Build quality was lamentable, even by 1988 standards, and it had a live rear axle and three-speed auto (both features eligible for heritage listing). The standard engine fitment was a 3.2-litre six that just couldn't be bothered.

Taurus – How did they think this droopy, half-melted, ovoid American had a place Down Under? The only joy was that it reminded us what the Falcon would look like if the Americans had it all their way, which they soon will.

Fairlane AU – This bulky 'town car' stumbled onto the stage in 1999 and the same sheet metal was still up there in 2007. By that time, the only takers were cabbies paying not a lot more than Falcon money. Ford Australia's great success of the 1960s and 1970s had been run completely into the ground.

Anglia – Ford is often very adventurous with its small cars (think Ka), and it sometimes works. This be-finned small car from 1959, though, didn't. Even the name suggests angles, of which the car had far too many and none of them pleasant.

Mustang – It appeared in Ford dealerships briefly in 2001, locally converted to right-hand drive and priced from $85,000. Yep, 85K for a car that was crude, pudgy, cramped, full of cheap plastics, none-too-quick and dodgy in the handling stakes. When someone paid full price, Ford rang a bell and held a little ceremony.

So, there. No arguments with any of that, is there?

Ford's awkward Anglia.

29 Just what is a Volvoid?

If you're a man, you'll probably have a quarter-life crisis. A couple of decades later, it will become uglier still.

The symptoms of this next big shift, according to *Addictionary* and other online 'new word' sources, will include a sudden lack of energy, crankiness and the overpowering urge to buy a showy sports car.

The term applied to this panicked reaction to middle age? *Menoporsche*.

The same expression is often applied to the offending vehicle itself, no matter what brand. For example: 'He's just bought a sleek new silver menoporsche'.

But is this the only new (or new-ish) motoring word around? Not at all.

The *Oxford American Dictionary* gave its 'Word of the Year' for 2008 to *hypermiling*, the art of deriving as much distance as possible from every drop of fuel.

Hypermiling may include such techniques as winding up the windows, turning off the air-conditioning, pumping the tyres to one kilopascal less than their exploding point and even coasting down hills in neutral (in the un-PC past, this last trick was commonly known by Americans as 'Mexican Overdrive').

The term 'range anxiety' also comes from the place that generates most other forms of anxiety, the United States.

An electric Mini …

If you've made it this far without using the term, you probably haven't driven an electric car. Range anxiety is defined by wordspy.com as 'Mental distress or uneasiness caused by concerns about running out of power while driving an electric car.'

Wordspy.com is a website created by Paul McFedries, a Canadian logophile. It has gathered up such delightful concepts as *dining al desko* (staying at your work station to eat your lunch) and *slactivism*. The latter is practised by people who want to make a difference, but couldn't be bothered going too far out of their way.

Cup-holder cuisine is another car-related term that has made its way onto the site, not least because US food companies now sell soup, drinkable yoghurt and even breakfast cereals in disposable containers designed to fit into standard cup-holders. Burger King's circular chip punnet is known as the *frypod*.

Cup-holder cuisine allows us to engage in *dashboard dining*, itself a necessity because of the increasing amount of *windshield time* we are all subject to.

Wordspy lists now include *Lexus Liberal* and *SUV Democrat* – mildly abusive terms for people known in other places and political systems as 'Bollinger Bolsheviks', 'Champagne Socialists' and 'members of the Limousine Left'.

More appealing is the term *Volvoid*. Wordspy traces it to *The New York Times* of 2004 as a description for a 'white, moderately affluent suburban professional who is politically liberal'. A *digi-necker* is 'a driver who slows down when passing an accident to take a picture of

... and an electric Th!nk from Norway.

the scene with a digital camera [blend of *digital* and *rubbernecker*]'. A *nanny car* 'uses computer technology to prevent the driver from making unsafe actions or decisions'. *Carcooning*? That's spending more and more time 'in auto'. *The Boston Globe* pointed out that homeless – though not car-less – residents of its city formed the Vehicularly Housed Residents' Association.

The Double Tongued Dictionary reveals some curious terms from the world of urban planning.

One is *teaser parking*, a small parking lot out the front of a store that looks ultra-convenient but, in reality, almost never has free spaces. Another is *naked road*. Stripped of all signs, signals, kerbs and traffic lights, such a thoroughfare is believed to encourage drivers to slow down and be more mindful of pedestrians.

People often say 'there's a big bottleneck on that road' when they mean 'there's a small bottleneck', which is much more of a problem. But the opposite of a road that loses lanes? A *neckout,* apparently.

Anyway, that's enough motor words for the moment. All that's left is to empty out the *carbage* (assorted passenger cabin flotsam and jetsam) from your *G-Machine* (a term invented by *Popular Science* for a car capable of producing more than 1 G in acceleration, braking and turning) and park it in your lavishly appointed – wait for it – *Garage Mahal*.

30 The equine origins of motor sport

Chariots provided the original horsepower-charged wheel-to-wheel combat.

When was this? No one knows for sure, though it's a fair bet that whoever built the world's second chariot challenged the builder of the world's first to a square-off.

Organised chariot racing was first described by Homer. The winner received a cauldron and a slave girl, the Ancient Greek equivalent of a silver cup and a pit-lane babe.

The early Olympics included chariot racing. The mantra then was presumably 'Citius, Altius, Deadlius'. Later it became 'Faster, Sillier, Fruitier' so that rhythmic gymnastics and synchronised diving could be included.

Chariot racing involved brave and skilful drivers, and transparent scrutineering. If the team claimed, say, three horsepower, there was an easy way to check.

The Romans took to the sport in a big way. Nero was said to have driven a chariot with ten horses. The famously excessive Heliogabalus tried elephants. Both emperors always won, even when they fell off.

Mere commoners usually made do with two or four neddies. Apparently, by adjusting the tethering of the inside animal(s), you could alter the steering to best suit the track, much like setting up a modern race car.

The Circus Maximus, the Monza of its day, attracted large and wild crowds decked in the colours of their teams. The teams worked together to block and even up-end opponents. It was common to force rivals into the safety fencing, which was made of bricks and marble for durability.

The racers wore helmets and carried a small knife to cut the reins if thrown out and dragged along. A whip was used to adjust the horse's throttle settings.

Both weapons were liable to be used on other competitors. However, many erroneous things people associate with chariot racing were framed by the 1959 film *Ben Hur*, starring gun-nut Charlton Heston.

Canadian writer Peter Donnelly suggests the film's heavy, elaborately decorated chariots would have been too slow.

'Surviving figurines and other representations show that the typical racing chariot was more like a basket on wheels. The driver stood on webbing that gave him a good, springy foothold.

'We can certainly dismiss as fiction, or even movie blooper, the idea of whirling blades extended from the hubs to chew up the opponents' spokes. Both chariots would surely be involved in calamity the instant any projection, rotating or not, came between the spokes of an opponent's wheel.'

KLAW & ERLANGER'S STUPENDOUS PRODUCTION

OF GENERAL LEW WALLACE'S

BEN·HUR

DRAMATIZED BY WILLIAM YOUNG MUSIC BY EDGAR STILLMAN KELLEY

BEN·HUR DRIVES SHEIK ILDERIM'S "STARS OF THE DESERT" TO VICTORY IN THE ANTIOCH CIRCUS, DEFEATING HIS ARCH-ENEMY MESSALA.

Life expectancy was low but Roman sportsmen earned big while it lasted. Gladiators hit such fiscal heights that Emperor Marcus Aurelius introduced a salary cap. According to Peter Struck, a Pennsylvania University classics professor, a Roman charioteer qualifies as the highest paid athlete of all time.

Gaius Appuleius Diocles, a Lusitanian Spaniard famed for his strong final dashes, won 1,462 of his 4,257 races. He survived an improbable twenty-four years at the top and amassed nearly 36 million sesterces in prize money.

Struck wrote that this was 'five times the earnings of the highest paid provincial governors over a similar period, enough to provide grain for the entire city of Rome for one year, or to pay all the ordinary soldiers of the Roman Army at the height of its imperial reach for a fifth of a year. By today's standards that last figure … would cash out to about $15 billion. Even without his dalliances, it is doubtful Tiger [Woods] could have matched it.'

After Rome fell, the sport remained popular in the Byzantine Empire. During AD 532 thousands were killed and half of Constantinople was burnt to the ground in weeklong riots surrounding a chariot race meet.

One of the motivations for the so-called Nika riots was a widespread belief that the results were fixed. Clearly that's where parallels with modern motor sport have to end. Such a thing could never happen now.

31 Any holiday advice?

'Before you head off on your holiday, it's important to make sure every aspect of your car is in peak condition,' says Dr Peter Pullman-Smithers, head of Administrative Facilities at DEF Insurance Brokers.

Dr Pullman-Smithers, a long-time road-safety advocate, has issued a fourteen-point checklist for drivers to get the most out of their holiday season. These points are:

- Tyres are of the utmost importance – they are your only connection with the road below. Make sure yours are completely bald. Any look at a race-car will demonstrate that treadless tyres offer more grip.
- Most petrol cars will run more efficiently on diesel. If you're not sure about your particular model, give it a go anyway.
- Most speedometers understate the true speed by about 40 per cent. Remind your P-plater relatives so they don't accidentally hold up any jolly holidaymakers keen to reach the beach.
- The rear parcel shelf can provide a convenient place for a young child to sleep during a long trip.
- If you've read this far, wow! I had assumed no one ever made it beyond the first paragraph, and so thought I could have a bit of fun for once. Then again, I'm a 'communications officer', according to my card, so what would I know? This is my ninth year of assembling

these stupid holiday season advice factoids, which Dr Pullman-Smithers doesn't even read, let alone write.

- Insurance companies allow up to one year's grace on premiums, so there's no reason to pay up until you have an accident.
- The breakdown lane provides a perfectly legal overtaking channel in certain conditions, such as when the motorist in front *just won't get on with it*.
- Administrative Facilities? Dr Smithers is head of Boring Services at this, the Tedious and Turgid Insurance Group. Not a real doctor, either; it's a finance PhD, probably from the University of the Internet. He thinks 'Dr' makes it seem he'd know about safety. He doesn't even know about insurance.
- Alcohol is a proven cure for car sickness. It improves reaction times too.
- A caravan or other heavy towed vehicle has the same effect as a Formula One wing, anchoring the rear end of the car to the road and allowing higher cornering speeds.
- Did I mention Dr PS is having a bit on the side? Not that there's anything wrong with that. It's entirely his business if he wants to lie to his wife and use company funds to take Roger to the annual Insurance Facility Administrators conference on the Gold Coast. Did I also mention I've just had my voluntary redundancy papers indelibly signed off?
- Maintain low coolant and oil levels. This saves weight, making the car more fuel efficient and helping the environment.
- There's a photo above his desk of the happy couple – Roger and the doctor – at Surfers in a rented Mini convertible, even though the

company hire policy clearly states 'Corolla or similar'. Not a seatbelt in sight, and their eyes are lit up like they've just hoovered an Omo box of Belushi. Long-time road-safety advocate indeed!

- Lastly, Australian Highway Patrol officers can now make EFTPOS transfers directly into their personal bank accounts. 'Considerations' are negotiable, but should be about half the traffic fine in question, with no loss of demerit points. It's perfectly legal, providing you raise the matter first. Tell them Peter Pullman-Smithers suggested it. He's a doctor, after all.

32 America the prolific

It's hard to say how many US carmakers there have been. Many small and obscure makes stumbled and fell before bringing even a single car to market, so it is almost impossible to ever complete a full list.

But it's fair to say there have been thousands and thousands of US carmakers. One attempt at completeness lists over 130 starting with the letter A.

However, if you want to remember the main defunct American autos, it's best to go back to the old Gilbert and Sullivan song. All together now …

I have a list of models from the automotive knackery
There's Hummer, Peerless, Plymouth and assorted other quackery
There's Tucker, Aerocar, DeLorean and Pontiac
There's Nash and Oakland, Hudson, Hupmobile and Frontenac

Pilgrim made no progress, and the same was true of Gadabout
AMC is RIP, and no one seems too sad about
The loss of Bricklin, Rugby too, and Kaiser, Durant, Reo
Oldsmobile, Duryea, Crosley, Dodgeson, and Geo

The Pierce Arrow

WITHOUT forgetting that, after all, a motor car is a piece of machinery, the Pierce Arrow has never failed to offer its owner the highest luxury also.

Here is the Pierce Runabout, the same effective Pierce chassis, fitted with a smaller body, combining all of the efficiency of the Pierce engine with the convenience of a runabout.

THE GEORGE N. PIERCE COMPANY, BUFFALO, N.Y.

PROMINENT NEW YORK BANKER, MR. STEPHEN BAKER, purchased the Pierce-Arrow pictured above in 1917. It is still one of the most important cars in his service.

PIERCE-ARROW

PIERCE ARROW 1931
You'd be perfectly at home on Fifth Avenue in this elegant 147-inch-wheelbase convertible sedan by LeBaron. Its engine was an L-head straight eight of 385 cubic inches developing 132 horsepower.

There's Willys-Knight and Overland, and Willys all alone
The Dixie Flyer didn't fly, the Eagle's long since flown
Farewell's been said to Auburn, Darrin, Duesenberg and Terraplane
Studebaker's dead as well as Brush and Bush and Ritz and Crane

Thomas tanked, and Rambler too, Whippet, Merz and Wolverine
Ideal was not, the Morse was shot, so too LaSalle and Heseltine
No mourning for Electra, nor for two cars known as National
Bye bye DeSoto, Packard, Stutz and others briefly fashionable

Unfortunately, lyricist W.S. Gilbert wound it up at that point, possibly sick of looking for triple rhymes among kaput American carmakers (let's be honest, some of the ones he chose were pretty far-fetched). Gilbert was probably also struggling with trying to see the future.

Still, he did pretty well for a man who died in 1911.

Brands he didn't mention include one-time big players such as Pierce-Arrow and Locomobile. Less known, but still known, were Marmon (one of the few companies to build a V16), Speedwell, Wharton, Victor, Rickenbacker, Remington, Simplex, Jackson, Mason, Merkel, Franklin, Frazer, Hoskins and Metropolitan.

Did we list Paige-Detroit, Buckmobile, Champion, Lexington, LaFayette or Miller? Neither did Gilbert.

There are plenty of expired American steam cars, the best known being Stanley Steamer, and a few brands that are now known for other things: General Electric, DuPont and Maytag.

Really daft names for now-reposing motors include Flexbi, Peter Pan, Gaylord, Browniekar and American Underslung (a name that referred to the car's low chassis). Details are scant, but there was also a Dodo. It was born and became extinct in 1912.

Deceased Americans named after places? Michigan, Niagara, Ohio, Madison, Columbia, Detroit (and Detroit Electric), Dixie, Springfield, Rochester and Cleveland.

The Columbus was named, presumably, after Christopher.

In terms of the cosmos, there was Saturn (from GM) and Mercury, the Ford divisional badge once plonked on the Australian-built Capri. At least four marques used the name Star, five used Comet, and six Meteor.

But for government help, Chrysler and GM would also push up daisies in this automotive graveyard. The Big Three would now be The Medium One.

ON HUMAN NATURE
33 Curious cases of hoarding

There's nothing wrong with hoarding, as long as you call it 'collecting'.

Collecting implies discriminating taste and abundant funds. And those who accumulate rare or expensive cars are often considered an upmarket strain of the collector breed.

However, use the term 'hoarding' and it comes with all the connotations of stinginess, paranoia and possibly a lonely death under toppling piles of accumulated tyres and dismantled engine blocks.

A highly hoardable 1932 Stutz Super Bear Cat.

Still, hoarders tend to fascinate. Hence those emails doing the rounds with real or imagined stories of barns opened for the first time in decades and discovered to contain rows of rare but completely neglected sports cars.

In 2009 a Bugatti Type 57S Atalante from 1937 was found in Newcastle in the UK, forty-eight years after it was mothballed and hidden by a reclusive English doctor. It was only one car, but it fetched €3.4 million at auction.

The wealthy Collyer brothers – Langley and Homer – managed to collect 130 tonnes of bric-a-brac (or 'vital supplies', as they might have put it) in their flash Fifth Avenue house on Manhattan during the first half of the twentieth century.

They weren't specifically car hoarders, though they had a complete Model T Ford in one room and tried to use its engine to power the house lights, thereby saving on electricity.

Australian motoring journalist John Wright published *My Other Wife is a Car*, a book dealing with the 130-plus cars he acquired in a spectacularly varied, and heroically unprofitable, series of exchanges.

Wright is a serial owner, however, rarely having more than a few at a time. He is also an enthusiastic driver. The most extreme hoarders would never consider driving their vehicles or, god forbid, culling them.

American millionaire Alexander Kennedy Miller, a gyrocopter-flying nutter, sorry eccentric, saved money by neglecting such things as home maintenance and personal grooming. After World War II he put most of the money he saved into bullion and old Stutzes. After his death in 1993, the various ramshackle barns on his property were found to contain thirty examples of this rare American sports/luxury

One of the many: author John Wright with his 1949 Jaguar Mark V.

marque, a Rolls-Royce or two and large numbers of precious metal ingots.

At least Miller had taste. Others have been known to obsessively collect Austin Allegros or Rambler Matadors.

The Schlumpf brothers also had discernment, even if it didn't extend to changing their gnome-like surname. Hans and Fritz were rich mill owners in Alsace when they started buying Bugattis in bulk. The marque had gone broke but they wrote to every known owner in the world offering to buy their cars.

Bugatti prices hadn't hit the great heights they would later achieve, but cornering the market was still a pricey business. It needed to be partly funded by cutting wages at the mill. Still, the eccentric brothers secretly built the world's largest and most valuable Bugatti collection and spent long hours simply gazing at it.

It was only when the pesky workers went on strike and broke into the locked rooms at the mill that the incredible scale of the 'Schlumpf collection' was revealed. It now forms the basis of the French National Motor Museum.

The Sultan of Brunei and family have bought a reputed 2000 cars through the years, many of them Rolls-Royces, Ferraris and other exotics, often expensively customised to their own eccentric tastes.

It may not quite count as hoarding, though leaked photos have shown what may or may not be many of the cars rotting in the basement car park of the family's 1700-room palace. Then again, most couldn't have been driven more than a few kilometres. The family isn't that big and spends much of its time overseas.

Still, when at home, a Sultan can't be expected to use Brunei's rather miserable public transport system.

His younger brother, Prince Jefri, didn't mind a boat or two either. He commissioned an ultra-luxurious motor launch named *Tits*, plus two tender boats, *Nipple 1* and *Nipple 2*.

Amazing what years of careful royal interbreeding can produce.

34 Is that a fact?

No. But just imagine if life were restricted to truths, home and otherwise. Whole sections of the Internet would disappear. Parliament and the advertising industry likewise. Only the media would be safe. No, really. Take it away:

- In 1959 Bob Jane, Ian 'Pete' Geoghegan and a team of six Sherpa guides completed the first successful ascent of Mount Panorama without supplementary oxygen.

- As well as building jet fighters, the original Saab company manufactured playing cards, drinking straws and garden furniture. The first Saab car, the 92, came about when an unusually long cold snap in Sweden decimated sales of barbecue settings and wrought iron benches.

- Every Lexus sedan has an acorn sealed in the hood lining to bring good luck to the buyer.

- The rock that Dick Johnston collided with at Bathurst, while leading the Hardie-Ferodo 1000 in 1980, has been preserved at the Australian National Museum. It's in a humidity-maintained glass cabinet next to a pair of long-nosed pliers once owned by Dame Nellie Melba.

- A long-wheelbase 'landau' version of the Facel Vega Facellia F-2 was once mass-produced on Christmas Island.

- Holden means 'armpit' in Finnish.
- The Russian-built Zil 101 limousine of 1938, produced at the height of Stalinist purges, came with the automotive world's first lifetime warranty. If it gave any trouble, you returned it to the Soviet government's complaint officers, and they killed you.
- The original prototype of the Citroën 2CV was so basic it didn't have a chassis. One of the occupants (ideally not the driver) had to lie in the starfish position and hold the axles.
- In parts of Wales, Volvos are banned after 9 p.m.
- Honda's smallest domestic car, the Uncle's New Maple Tree 450 Turbo, has been released in many versions including the Mary of Magdalene Edition. Aimed at Christians, who make up between 1 and 2 per cent of the Japanese population, it comes with two-tone 'Lourdes' upholstery and a 'Pope on a Rope' rear-view mirror ornament.
- In 1976 Wayne Goss became the first man – and is still the only Queensland premier – to win both the Australian Grand Prix and the annual Bathurst Enduro. Ford celebrated this feat by producing a limited-production Falcon coupé known as the Wayne Goss Special. It featured a 302 V8 and a bonnet mural depicting the official Queensland state aquatic symbol, the Barrier Reef Anemone fish.
- Modern lane-keeping systems – which can steer the car back on course if the driver loses attention – require so much 'brain power' they quickly become bored. Researchers have found examples of rogue systems deliberately and randomly braking one wheel to send cars out of line and give themselves something to do.

35 The pain of loving a man who might die

'They are fighting each other,' says the head-shaking Formula One team manager, 'and not the road.'

'It hurts,' the suitably leggy blonde gasps in another scene, 'to love a man who could be dead next week.'

So what is it about motor racing films that brings out the worst in dialogue writers?

The film in question here, *The Young Racers*, has the irresistible catch line: 'They treated beautiful women as if they were fast cars … ROUGH!'

It was made in 1963 and is widely considered one of the better films by director Roger Corman. Even better, some say, than *Swamp Women.* (A measure of the man-as-artist: Corman supposedly won a bet by getting one of his feature films, *The Little Shop of Horrors*, in the can in under three days.)

None of the Young Racers look very young. What they do look, with their slicked-back dark hair, is remarkably similar. Perhaps that's why there's frequent addressing of the characters by name.

William Campbell plays American Joe Machin, a Grand Prix driver who is selfish, conceited and arrogant. It's fiction of course.

Mark Damon plays Stephen Children, a journalist writing a book about Machin, mainly as revenge because the selfish, conceited and arrogant Machin had treated Children's girlfriend as if she were a fast car.

Weirdly, Mark Damon's voice was dubbed by William Shatner, a man famous for playing Captain Kirk in *Star Trek* and for producing some of the most execrable singing ever captured by recording technology.

The plot thickens when Machin's teammate is taken ill and the Lotus boss asks Children to drive the second car. That may sound completely ludicrous, but we journalists know it happens.

'Help us out, one of you guys,' I've so often heard the likes of McLaren's Ron Dennis yell into the press tent, 'Jensen's running a bit of a temperature.'

If not for happy little quirks of fate like that, an unassuming wordsmith like me might never have secured pole at Monaco or overtaken a double world champ flat out through Spa's Eau Rouge. But I digress.

Some other curios surrounding this film: Francis Ford Coppola was second unit director, while Jim Clark and Bruce McLaren helped out in the driving scenes. There's some good moving footage too, as if they've taken a few cars out and followed a camera car before or after the real race.

Neither McLaren nor Clark scored a screen credit, although the Kiwi was constantly mentioned by the 'track' commentators and even credited with winning a race ahead of the two film leads in their Lotuses.

As you'd expect, there are lots of exotic locales, plus attractive cars and expensive women (or were those two the other way around?). There's also behaviour consistent with the time. The drivers go for a boozy meal the night before the race, and follow it with some good old-fashioned drink-driving with the steering wheel in one hand and champagne in the other.

Some of the real Grand Prix footage is wonderful, but there's often clumsily spliced-in footage (usually of prangs) from other races, categories and circuits.

Still, we see F1 cars wildly oversteering at Monaco and Spa, back in the days when the movie poster – 'A little death each day, a lot of love every night' – wasn't a complete exaggeration.

That's probably a reason they don't make modern GP films. The slogans just wouldn't cut it: 'A lot of promotional appearances each day, a nutritionally balanced meal and an early bedtime every night.'

36 Colonel Gaddafi and his Rocket

There was quite a kerfuffle about the expensive cars pulled out of the various Gaddafi family mansions after the 2011 overthrow of the despised Libyan leader Muammar Gaddafi.

They included a white Lamborghini and, less obviously, a Fiat 500.

The most interesting vehicle, however, never surfaced. It was Colonel Gaddafi's self-designed Rocket.

Not that the Fiat, a rather bizarre open-sided electric version, wasn't interesting. The bright spark who commissioned it perhaps didn't consider the implications of having no doors in a country that is, broadly speaking, an oven filled with sand.

By one report, the US$130,000 electric Fiat had a separate petrol engine to power the air-conditioning, arguably diminishing any environmental gains.

Muammar Gaddafi's interest in cars went beyond a pointlessly modified Fiat. He fancied himself as a designer, unveiling the Saroukh el-Jamahiriya, or Libyan Rocket, in 1999.

It was a five-seater, wedge-shaped sedan measuring a substantial 5.5 metres from end to end and finished in a fetching shade of Revolutionary Green.

The car: Libyan Rocket.
The man: Muammar Gaddafi.

The Rocket was described as the safest car in the world and, lest anyone should think its designer was, say, a delusionary, murderous wing nut, the spokesman added that Gaddafi spent long hours thinking of 'ways to preserve human life all over the world'. Among the lightly explained innovations was an 'electronic defence system,' and a device to cut the fuel supply during an accident to prevent fire. High-tech or what?

The most unusual safety feature was a pointed nose to ensure that during a head-on collision the Rocket would slide past the oncoming car. The limitation with this otherwise brilliant idea was that the other car would have to be another Rocket, and at that stage, there wasn't one.

Still, the BBC reported a new factory in Tripoli would start production by October 1999. Unsurprisingly, it didn't. The idea was largely forgotten until an African Union summit in 2009, during which the Colonel did the old Rocket trick a second time around.

He wheeled out an updated but similar vehicle and almost exactly the same gushing quotes were offered by almost exactly the same official spokesman (well, he was ten years older).

Mr Dukhali al-Meghareff seemed to have done a search-and-replace on his old press release. He announced – again – that the Rocket was the world's safest car and 'proof that the Libyan revolution is built on the happiness of man'. This time around the vehicle was built in Italy not Tripoli, but it wasn't a great deal less ugly. The nose was even more pointed, and the tail was now super-sharp too, perhaps in case you reversed into another Rocket.

The run-flat tyres were apparently good for hundreds of kilometres when deflated, while interior materials included uniquely Libyan leathers, fabrics and marbles. Yep, marbles.

The main focus was still safety, with warm, cuddly Muammar G apparently worried about the high number of fatalities on Libyan roads (rather than in Libyan political prisons). Plans were announced – sorry, re-announced – to put the Rocket into production.

Meanwhile, Turin-based Tesco TS SpA, a company undertaking design and engineering work for major carmakers, was brave enough to stick up its corporate hands and say, 'Yep, we built it.'

According to the company's Italian language website – as told to Google Translate – the 'authorship and style concept is due to Colonel Muammar Gaddafi in person,' while the car is 'dedicated to celebrating the visionary talent of the opulence of a head of state'. Tesco also confirmed the Rocket as a real running prototype. However, the company wouldn't confirm the origin of the platform nor the 3-litre V6 engine.

If anyone does find the Rocket, perhaps we'll find out more about that 'electronic defence system'. Maybe that's the real origin of the car's name.

37 What do people say when they complain?

Dear Sir,

I wish to politely and humbly express my deep-seated dismay at your recent review of the Trundle 75.

I have owned one of these magnificent automobiles for fourteen months and have never experienced the problems you mentioned in your biased, inaccurate and downright stupid review, you nasty little creep.

My car achieves consistently better consumption than the 50 L/100 km official combined fuel cycle, yet you kept returning to those almost irrelevant laboratory-derived figures. The simple fact is that any half-decent driver can improve on those lab results by turning off the engine on downhill runs and not using the electrical accessories.

Your sloppily crafted article also criticised the engine, specifically its tendency to explode, punching holes in the bodywork and ventilating passers-by with small shards of hot metal. Yet not once did you mention

Dear Sir,

that all Trundle cars now come with 24-hour (per week)
roadside assistance, with no cap on usage.

I took advantage of this VIP service just yesterday
and the ambulance and tow-truck people were cheerful and
friendly. The Trundle courtesy vehicle – which is clean,
well maintained and has three-speed derailleur gears – is
mine until my own machine is fixed, even if it takes years.

So much for your lie about the company not caring for
its customers.

You wrote that 'the exterior styling treatment is
unresolved'. What is unresolved about it, you fancy-pantsy

bloviating gasbag? The bodywork is smooth, it covers all the mechanical parts, except for a small part of the engine, and doesn't leak, except during inclement weather.

Why not praise the innovation of combining a high nose with a low tail and passenger doors that are hinged at the bottom?

Why? Because 'unresolved' is your snarky euphemism for 'ugly'. In other words you are putting your own trendy pinko-gayo inner-city tastes ahead of the aesthetic judgement of Trundle buyers, whose average age (78.6 years according to the latest owners' survey) shows they've been around the traps a lot longer than slobbering moronic toddlers like you.

You also wrote in your superior, condescending way that the steering system 'at times completely refuses to operate'. This is a gross exaggeration. The steering diminution – not loss – that you slyly alluded to has happened to me only once in nearly 9000 kilometres. And absolutely no one suffered. It was all pretty instantaneous really.

The Trundle Corporation fully acknowledged this minor technical problem just before relocating its headquarters next to James Hardie's in Burkina Faso.

And, as you'd also know, if you weren't a truckling parvenu with a penchant for farmyard animals, Trundle has since introduced a new steering system that incorporates both a rack and a pinion.

Owners can receive a free upgrade by taking their car to the impressive new facilities in Ouagadougou and waiting the required thirty to forty days. Any legal issues can be dealt with by the Burkinabé Consumer Affairs Department.

This is not the inefficient and corrupt organisation you suggested in your odious commentary, you scrofulous burke. Their Complaint Facilitation Fees are entirely reasonable and can be paid - indeed, must be paid - in unmarked US bills.

I suspect your alarmist, spiteful story was paid for by Trundle's competitors, who have much to fear from the forthcoming 75B model. The story will surely cut into the brand's retained value, which is already down to 7 per cent thanks to alleged journalists like you. Why should we loyal Trundle owners have to suffer further financial hardship?

Anyway that's it. I just wanted to politely express a few thoughts and set some things straight.

None of it should be taken personally. After all, but for the grace of God, I too could have been stupid, pompous and plain wrong about everything. And I too could be working for the loathsome organ that you use to disseminate untruths.

Up yours sincerely,

Albert Hackney-Grumble-Smith.

RATTLETRAPS, ETC.
38 Other locals that deserve a thump

Henry and The General weren't the only mainstream players to make cars here. What about Toyota, Nissan Chrysler/Mitsubishi, and BMC/Leyland? Yes, there's been a pox or two from those houses – such as:

Austin X6 – There were Kimberley and Tasman versions, depending on whether you preferred cyanide or arsenic. Cramming an optional straight six into this front-drive car was a brave but pointless move. It

The Kimberley in its natural state: beside the road.

Chrysler by Chrysler.

didn't help that the six was thirsty and unreliable, or that the car itself was underdeveloped and badly made. But you knew that – it was made by Leyland.

Morris Marina – Ohmigod! Who'd have thought it possible to make something this odious using only metal, glass and plastic? It was meant to be a rugged and reliable alternative to the above, but was neither. The only way to make things worse would be to add the P76's six-cylinder engine. So they added it.

Leyland P76 – It could have been good. But it wasn't. We could go on. That would be more than most P76s did.

Chrysler (by Chrysler) – An early 1970s luxury car that nobody needed, built by a company that – hey, Charger aside – seemed to have lost all clue. The name was daft (by daft).

Valiant VH Hardtop – The heavy, thirsty, flabby 1971 Hardtop was bigger than the already obese VH sedan, for goodness sake. Yet rear legroom was close to zero. If you wanted a Valiant coupe, why not the vastly superior Charger?

Toyota Camry Hybrid – Built on the wishful principle that do-gooders want to do their good anonymously. If only they'd put a windmill on the roof ...

Toyota Avalon – It was supposed to be the Centaur, but the name had to change, rather like Britain's royal family had to become Windsor during WWI instead of Saxe-Coburg-Goering-Luftwaffe, or whatever it was. Someone realised *Centaur* was an Australian hospital ship war-criminally torpedoed by the Japanese. The car itself was a dated piece of droopiness aimed at the American market. Although no one bought it, it served one purpose: it made the Camry look stylish.

Datsun 200B – People bought Japanese-sourced cars in the late 1970s because they were reliable, economical and relatively refined. No one knows, then, why they bought the 200B. Having fooled the public initially, Nissan Australia cranked up production just in time for the public to wake up. Oops.

Toyota Corona 'Starfire' – Although unspeakably dull, the Corona was ultra-reliable. This attribute was comprehensively undone by installing a Holden Starfire engine in 1979 to lift local content. Toyota

Yes, it is a Nissan.

engineers made dozens of changes to this six-cut-back-to-four, but it didn't help. As the saying goes, you can't polish a Starfire.

Austin Freeway – One of many 'pre-76' attempts to build a local BMC/Leyland six. This dated, be-finned parts-bin special sold fewer in all of 1963 than the EH Holden sold every week. Deservedly, too.

Nissan Pintara – It is not true that Pintara is an Arrernte Aboriginal word meaning 'tedious, dated Japanese fare unconvincingly reheated' (or indeed that Linguists believe German is the only other language that has a single word for it). However, in sedan form, Nissan Australia's 1989 effort was dreary, while the locally developed Superhatch hunchback, sorry hatchback, was meant to bring to mind the Audi Avant. It did, as in 'get me an Audi Avant so I can drive as far away from this thing as possible'.

Nissan Ute – Ford tried to flog a version of the Pintara known as Corsair. The *quid pro quo* was a bog-standard 1988 Falcon ute with a Nissan sticker on the nose and tailgate. If you didn't laugh at the silliness, you'd have to cry.

Mitsubishi 380 – It wasn't bad, just unnecessary. They built it (in 2005) in the vain hope that the people would come. 'Hello … hello, is anyone there?'

The P76 makes its sheepish debut.

Bufori Geneva – OK, Bufori isn't a main player. It isn't even strictly an Australian car these days. But it certainly has caused some comment. Bufori started off in Australia, building a version of the US-designed Madison kit-car. This morphed into something uniquely, er, Bufori. The company moved to Malaysia, where the Geneva was developed, perhaps with help from people in the costume jewellery industry. According to the official guff, 'The name BUFORI does not have any essential meaning, but rather stands for B – Beautiful, U – Unique, F – Fantastic, O – Original, R – Romantic, I – Irresistible.'

Bufori's Geneva.

39 Other fuels for thought

People have run cars on all manner of things: coconuts, cooking oil, methane, chicken fat, palm oil, sawdust, producer gas, hydrogen, beer and spirits.

Biofuel made from fast-growing switchgrass has been dubbed *grassoline*, and presumably the ethanol now being derived from household waste (and tipped by some as a future automotive fuel) will be *trasholine*.

A few years ago the Ananova news agency reported that German inventor Dr Christian Koch had found a way to turn dead cats into cheap 'high-quality bio-diesel'. The story – apparently cribbed from a German language report in *Bild* newspaper – said that Koch had calculated that a fully grown feline could yield 2.5 litres of fuel, so it would take about twenty dead cats for a fill-up.

In a cruel blow for sensationalist journalists everywhere, the doctor soon denied he'd ever specified putting mini tigers in the tank.

'I use paper, plastics, textiles and rubbish,' Koch told Reuters.

'… I've never used cats and would never think of that. At most the odd toad may have jumped in.'

Ambitious ways of powering family cars have included solar (not very quick), nuclear (not very welcome in most streets) and wind (not very reliable).

When this writer was editing a motoring publication many years ago, a man who called himself an inventor asked us to write a reverential piece about his brilliantly conceived, zero-emission, fuel-free, air-powered car.

This was not a compressed-air car, as has been demonstrated by French maker MDI and some others. Indeed it wasn't a car at all, it was a piece of paper with a simple pencil drawing on it and the words 'Patent Pending' and 'Copyright' written in every other available space.

The 'car' was shown in cross section. It had a big opening at the front and a propeller inside. The air coming in the front was funnelled to turn the propeller blades, which in turn rotated the wheels.

Where did the moving air come from? From the speed of the car, of course. And how did the car acquire that speed? Er, from the fan.

Other inventors have harnessed wind power in more practical ways, though never sufficiently efficiently. Most commuters don't like the risk of being becalmed.

Early wind power: *Wagon of Fools* by Hendrik Gerritsz Pot, circa 1640.

Anyway, isn't everything going electric? Seems so. For the first time since the 1970s, every carmaker and his wife have an electric vehicle under development. Of course many of these 'pure electrics' should be called 'coal powered cars' or, in some countries, 'nuclear powered cars'.

This is because batteries aren't a power source. They merely allow the oomph from elsewhere to be stored in a relatively inefficient manner until you wish to use it. Such cars aren't emission free; proponents of same need to word their sentences ornately with such phrases as 'no local emissions'.

Obviously there are advantages in having no tailpipe emissions, especially in urban areas, and hopefully we'll soon be providing the sparks for these new electric cars with solar, hydro, wind, tidal and things we haven't even thought of yet.

In the meantime a 'coal powered car' sounds a fair bit less clean, green and charge-a-premium-able.

Another claimed advantage of electricity is that it is cheap. A similar advantage is claimed for used cooking oil and every other alternative wonder fuel. This misses the point that while *grassoline, trasholine* or even *kitty litres* might be cheaper than gasoline, gasoline is also cheaper than gasoline.

It's the producer cartels, profit-taking resellers and government taxers right along the chain that make it the price it is. You can be damn sure if something replaces normal everyday petrol, then that same something will be ratcheted up then taxed to exactly the same hilt.

There's no such thing as a free ride.

40 Could PR be worse?

'Hello, my name is Trixie and I'm calling to check that you received our email about the brand-new lifetime guarantee on all WonderSparkle automotive paint protection products …'

'Ken here from Badger & Badger Media Professionals. We sent you a press release on a new range of seat covers. I need to find out when it will appear in the newspaper because the client wants to know.'

'Hi, Fifi from Up to the Minute PR Solutions. Just ringing to check that you are still deputy editor of the paper's Quadricycle and Steamcar section.'

'Richard here. Mate … mate … how they hanging? Thought I'd give you a heads up that I'm about to send out a photo of an advanced sketch of the new body kit we're planning to make available for SUVs. Mate, mate, *maaate* …'

'Am I speaking to Tommy from *The Daily Telegraph* … oh, no, sorry *Herald*, but you are in the same group, aren't you? Anyway, like, Bryce here from The Media Experts and I'm like ringing to let you know that the managing director of Super Safety Workshops is like available for interview to talk about the need to have shock absorbers regularly tested … sorry, did you just fall over?'

OK, you get the picture. This is the age of spin, and traction control isn't helping one little bit.

The diversity of this low-grade urging is one thing. Far more astounding is the sheer number of people representing external agencies no one's ever heard of trying to spruik fringe products and services.

The sole talent of at least some of these people is an ability to demonstrate in just a few words that they know absolutely nothing whatsoever about the media. Nor, quite obviously, do they have a clue about the type of article readers are likely to find in a given publication, having clearly never, ever read it.

Not that I feel strongly about these … dills. I mean, if the unqualified and unimaginative can call themselves media experts and drag money from people who know as much as they do about something they're both in the dark about, well, good luck to them.

Major carmakers tend to employ people with media experience and anyway, there are only fifty or so car brands. It's the parallel world of PR puff-houses that seems to involve millions. Emails can be quickly binned. But anyone who's worked in a newsroom knows the blight of the follow-up phone call. *Of course your unsolicited, unwanted email has been received! I would have rung you if it hadn't!*

Sometimes there's the pretence that the call is to check whether you require more information … than the information you already have and don't need. And what's the angle of most of these press releases? Broadly speaking:

- The product or service is new and that makes it interesting. Indeed, worthy of an eight-page colour wraparound in your publication.
- The product or service is associated with something or someone said to be interesting. A sporting team, for example, or some tiresome rent-a-quote, or the entire cast of The Biggest Self-Abuser.

- It has miracle properties. It can defy gravity, stop global warming, cut your motoring bills by 90 per cent, or make a Camry attractive.
- It's the 'fastest growing', 'exported around the world', 'voted most popular in a recent online poll' or vastly successful by some immeasurable and irrelevant metric.
- The product or service is righting wrongs and/or part of a picture broader than you might imagine. For example, toe-stubbings caused by poor lighting in automotive foot-wells cost the Australian economy over $2 billion last year, says the managing director of a new locally designed system that improves lighting in automotive foot-wells.

Actually, Fifi, when we said there was no chance of your automotive foot-well lighting enhancement system copping a mention in print, we were wrong. It just did.

41 Yesterday's view of tomorrow

In *The Glass Canoe*, a David Ireland novel that is set pretty well entirely within an Australian pub, a bloke named Alky Jack roars a whole lot of apparent rubbish about computers: 'One day they'll … even be in charge of your car so you can't drive through a red light or crash into someone or change lanes if there's a car alongside you.'

The Glass Canoe was written in 1976 when a Holden Kingswood HX was considered pretty nifty and the first Apple hadn't dropped from the tree. Yet Alky Jack clearly had a better idea about what was coming than most futurists. Sober or otherwise.

Predictions about the next big thing in cars are almost as old as cars themselves. Take *Illustrated World*, April 1917: 'The aeroautocraft of the future will roll on the road, cleave through the water, fly through the air. Its owner will start from his garage or hangar, travel streets or roads at will, cross streams or lakes that lie in his path, rise in the air and fly over a hill, a valley, or woods, to another road, all at his pleasure.'

And how will such a vehicle be powered? Hydro power, delivered wirelessly. *Modern Mechanix* predicted in 1932 that cars would be guided by radio, and would beep loudly if you turned into the wrong road. The same magazine, soon after, said the car of the future would

One wheel good, four wheels bad.

be greatly fortified, 'so strong that no ordinary collision could best it'. The better known *Popular Science* told us, in July 1946, that 'rocket propellants, cased in special jet housings under the hood,' would provide spectacularly efficient emergency brakes. On an icy highway, a vehicle with these brakes would stop in a fifth the distance of a normal car.

Four years later, special brakes seemed less important to *Popular Science* editors because, within fifty years, the average family would use their teardrop-shaped car (powered by denatured alcohol) only for short journeys. Most trips would be taken in the family helicopter, stored on the roof of the house.

Science Digest, in April 1958, presented what is perhaps yesterday's most pervading image of tomorrow, aside from the flying car: 'When you drive onto a superhighway, you'll reach over to your dashboard and push the button marked "Electronic Drive". Selecting your lane, you'll settle back to enjoy the ride as your car adjusts itself to the prescribed speed. You may prefer to read or carry on a conversation with your passengers – or even catch up on your office work.'

Ten years later, *Mechanix Illustrated* presented a major treatise on how we'd be getting about in 2008. It mentioned that private cars would be banned inside most city centres, with 'moving sidewalks and electratrams' providing the transport.

Between cities, you guessed it: you'd be leaning back and reading the paper 'on a flat TV screen over the car's dashboard. Tapping a button changes the page.'

Your car would touch 150 mph in the city's suburbs, then hit '250 mph in less built-up areas, gliding over the smooth plastic road [while] the traffic computer … keeps vehicles at least 50 yards apart'. Nearby would be the 'launching pad from which 200-passenger rockets blast off for other continents'. Other popular vacation destinations would include undersea resorts and 'hotel satellites'. There'd be plenty of time for holidays too (and for reading daft predictions by people who don't have a clue), because the average working day would be a mere four hours.

42 Do Greeks make cars?

If you listen to the Euro-critics, the only thing the Greeks make is trouble for those hardworking French and virtuous, never-give-anyone-a-moment's-bother Germans.

But the country has a long and noble tradition of wheeled human transport going back at least as far as the Trojan Horse.

Modern car making started in the early years of the twentieth century and has given us such unforgettable cars as, OK, the names have slipped my mind for the moment but they'll come back.

The Dim. That's right, that's one of them. It was the unfortunate result of Mr Georgios Dimitriadis shortening his name to create the Dim Motor Company.

Hopes were high. After all, Mr D had been connected to Greece's mildly successful Bioplastic Attica three-wheeler of the 1960s. But the new venture crumbled circa 1982 after about ten vehicles were made.

Namco built some very boxy-looking off-roaders in the 1970s and 1980s. Many were based on Citroëns. Some were badged as Citroëns, while MAVA built a unique Greek utility labelled as a Renault.

Mebea adapted Reliant designs. Which was courageous. Someone else did Alfa 33s, which was even more venturesome.

The Neorian Chicago.
Enough said.

The 1960s saw a boom in Greek microcars (there were several sold alongside the Bioplastic ones). Most had three wheels; some had 50 cc engines to give Peel-like performance.

That trend was broken by the Tzen. It was a pretty good-looking, Dino-esque coupe styled by a Greek architect and running a Saab engine. Production, though, totalled somewhere between hardly any and not very many.

There have been far more producers of busses and trucks than cars in Greece, partly because of prohibitive taxes on passenger vehicles at various times, bureaucracy that owed a lot to the area's Byzantine forebears, and a distinct lack of folding stuff among the general population.

When the general population finally did get plenty of folding stuff, thanks largely to the Euro currency and easy credit, they wanted Porsches and Benzes, not Dims and Namcos. And, after years of forced automotive restraint, they bought them in bulk.

If the Greek industry had a nadir, it would have to be the Neorion Chicago of 1974. It was a big, luxurious sedan, fitted with a Jeep V8 engine and four-wheel drive. However, its squared-off bodywork was adorned with a chromed grille the size and shape of an industrial oven and old-fashioned running boards. Oblong headlights on stalks finished it all off aptly.

The designer, Georgios Michael, apparently blamed the company CEO for interfering with his beautiful design and creating a 'mountain dinosaur'. One generously forgiving web contributor recently wrote that the modern penchant for both retro and luxury 4WDs demonstrates that the Chicago was ahead of its time.

That's a long stretch. Just because others produced cars that were ugly and pointless afterwards, doesn't mean the Chicago was prescient. It just means the others were ugly, pointless *and* late.

Anyway, only two Chicagos were sold, with the makers blaming changes in legislation. The fuel crisis of the time can't have helped either.

There was much more promise in the sports cars built by Vassileios Scavas. Mark One came out in 1973. It never made it into production, despite having gullwing doors and looking refreshingly modern and svelte – if you chose the viewing angle very carefully.

Mark Two, a more integrated effort (and also with gullwing doors), was first seen in 1992 but fell at the first bureaucratic hurdle, which Greek authorities chose to place about 4 miles high.

There are no cars built in Greece today in any serious volumes. Not even in any mildly amusing volumes. One European automotive body states there are fewer than 3000 people employed in automotive manufacturing in Greece, mostly turning out spare parts.

A car-led recovery is not expected any time soon.

43 The worst car film . . . ever

There have been many claimants to the title, including Sly Stallone's *Driven*.

However, the racks of the suburban video store may have unveiled something worse.

Now, one should never, ever rent a film with the quote 'Hot cars and hotter women' written across the box. It's one of those simple rules, like not googling 'Best Way To Dispose Of A Body' on your work computer.

But this writer did rent such a film with such a quote, albeit purely in the course of anthropologic study. It was *Redline*, 'presented by Daniel Sadek' who also came up with the story.

Bizarrely, the opening shot was of a skyscraper adorned with a neon sign saying 'Quick Loan Funding'. It was a mighty odd opening for a car film but also the first sign that *Redline* is more interesting than the average crap film – and more crap, too. There's more story behind the film than *in* it, and we'll come to that shortly.

The narrator is Natasha, top-notch mechanic and singer in the 'hottest unsigned band on the West Coast'. Her motor-sport legend of a father died in a racing accident and she's promised her mother she will never race, despite being, quite obviously, the most brilliant driver around.

Natasha's voiceover introduces a group of cardboard cutout characters, explaining their characteristics so that the narrative doesn't have to demonstrate them. They're a bunch of wealthy wastrels who bet on private races involving exotic cars, presumably to ease the ennui of having it all.

To fit more clichés in, you'd need to extend the length of the film.

All the obvious cars are included: Ferraris, Lambos, Cobras, Corvettes, Porsches and so on, though the Bugatti Veyron probably arrived too late.

There's a Maybach limousine too, and it could be driven sideways through the gaps in plot and continuity.

Unlikely looking racing, on street and strip, is separated by ample crashes and ghastly acting and plot points.

Sadek generously provided so much work for such a large number of young actresses that there wasn't enough budget left to fully dress them.

It all finishes – rather than, say, climaxes – with the assembled bozos putting up a $100 million pot for a race involving a Porsche Carrera GT, McLaren SLR, a US-built Saleen S7 and a Ferrari Enzo.

One of the cars is driven by – *drum roll, drum roll* – Natasha. But you guessed that, didn't you?

The mystery of why her band is unsigned is solved when she sings a song as pre-race entertainment. It starts with the words: *I want to be your car tonight, so you can take me for a ride.* I suspect the song was Danny Sadek's idea too.

So who is Sadek? An American money-man who made kazillions, which he used to buy a large collection of cars. And what better way to show them off than in a $33-million filmic folly?

I'm not going to suggest that everyone in the finance industry is a beady-eyed charlatan. In fact, many of them have entirely regular eyes. But Sadek's speciality was loading up 'subprime' customers with monstrous loans at punitive rates. He worked out of California where, according to *The Orange County Register*, it was easier to gain a licence to be a money-lender than a barber (cutting hair required 1500 hours of training).

The neon sign was meant to plug Sadek's loathsome business but, by the time the film came out in 2007, Quick Loan Funding had gone belly-up and Sadek's cars had been flogged off.

To complete the picture, so to speak, *Redline* was roasted by critics and earned back only a tiny fraction of its costs.

Sadek was the intended target of a violent home invasion in 2009. By then his reported debts totalled $1.5 billion. As the *Redline* trailer said: 'When you are in this deep, the only way out is to cross the line.'

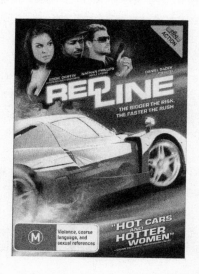

44 What would Enid write?

I say, this is going to boil up into a jolly adventure, isn't it, driving a new British car for a review.

What ho! With the summer hols not that far away, boys and girls, it seems only right to ask me, the author of 800 children's books, to review the new Jaguar.

This is the big one – the badges call it an XJ – and the styling, although a little modern, has the Mrs Blyton seal of approval.

Inside, the leather seating is delumptious, and there are lashings of chrome and wood, and shiny bright buttons that do all sorts of magic things.

The ignition is keyless – a secret code is not needed, which is a jolly shame because that would be mighty good fun. Never fear. There is a map, and a compass too, hidden away in the clever little screen in the centre of the dashboard. That makes this car just right for all sorts of adventures.

Is it fast? Rather! I'm told that the 3-litre six-cylinder is completely new. It is super-charged, while I am sure most of the conveyances made by those Continental types and sooty people across the seas have engines that are normal-charged.

The XJ is roomy, with loads and loads of space for Peter and Janet

Enid Blyton, possibly finishing her latest roadtest.

and Jack and Barbara and George and Pam and Colin and Susie and Binkie too.

Scamper, though, would have left fur on the deep-pile carpet. So he had to be put down.

One created quite a scene when one drove around in this enchanting new motor. Even Old Pete, the village's dusky but harmless old cripple, waved as we drove past.

'H-H-Hello, Enid,' he stuttered. 'Hello, Peter and Janet and Jack and Barbara and George and Pam and Colin and Susie and Binkie too. Where's Scamper?'

We all waved back. 'Watch out, Old Pete – oops!' the children laughed as he turned around and collided with the postman, sending the postman and his bicycle through a marvellously tall hedge.

The post is brought by a Chinaman now, so more giggles all round!

The Jaguar's steering and springing is grand. We were able to sharply swerve at speed around Mr Tipple, stumbling out of the Faraway Tree Alehouse. If we hadn't clipped him with the passenger side wing mirror, he'd have no broken bones at all.

'Silly Mr Tipple,' the children said sternly at the prone form of a man they knew would never travel in a Jaguar because he's not prepared to work hard and take responsibility for his own life. And is working class.

The XJ is a big, strong car for boys. Now they have up-to-date styling, perhaps one day the company will be extra modern and make a little, gentle car for girls to use when they are not cooking, cleaning or being gender stereotyped.

The only teensy-weensy problem with the last Jaguar I drove was an angry pixie under the bonnet. The press department has assured me that although Jaguars had some quality problems in the past, they're now absolutely tip-top. See, I'm not the only one working in fiction. (I'm joking, of course. Or would be, if I had even the slightest sense of humour.)

There's only one other fly in the ointment. I read on the new-fangled wikinet-googleweb that there are some Indians involved with the Jaguar company.

I'm not sure how people from this queer land, with their sneaky foreign ways, can contribute. But there you have it.

45 What is hyperlink hell?

Journalism, as Mark Twain or someone else once quipped, is 30 per cent inspiration and 70 per cent staying away from the Internet.

Which brings us to hyperlink hell. It's a term for when you set out to write a motoring column and decide to quickly look up, say, 'turbocharger'.

You just need to confirm the year the turbo first appeared in mainstream road cars. You think it was the Chevrolet Corvair, circa 1962, but you see the claim that it was actually the Oldsmobile Turbo Jetfire.

The Jetfire is a car you remember had a reputation for producing more fire than jet. You read more. For a brief moment you feel nostalgic about Oldsmobile, formed in 1897, but later stripped, looted and killed by GM.

You click on the link. The rot has already set in.

The founder of Oldsmobile was one of the few men to give his name (or variations thereof) to two brands of car and a rock band. He was Ransom Eli Olds, son of Pliny Fiske Olds and daughter of Sarah Whipple Olds. Who named these people?

And hey, wasn't the aluminium 215 V8 engine in the Turbo Jetfire the same block used in the world-conquering Repco-Brabham? Better check that.

Nash Metropolitan.

This leads you to the racing car company, reading beyond the Jack Brabham–Ron Tauranac partnership and on to later owner Bernie Ecclestone, who said: 'Women should be dressed in white like all the other kitchen appliances.' His comment was aimed at Danica Patrick. What was her best place in the Indy 500? Click. Third in 2009.

Patrick finished just behind poor Dan Wheldon who, two years later, became the fifth driver to die in a racing car in the same year he won the Indy 500.

Another of the five was Gaston Chevrolet (1920). Gaston's older brother, Louis, co-founded the car company bearing the family name in 1911 with former General Motors head William C. Durant. Then Durant used the success of the new company to regain control of GM in 1916 (Louis was jettisoned and, a click or two will tell you, died penniless).

When Durant re-joined GM, he sacked Charles Nash, who went on to form Nash Motors. Which merged with Kelvinator in 1937. Hey, that's worth looking up.

Company founder Kiichiro Toyoda in bronze, Toyota City.

Nash-Kelvinator itself merged with another entity, the Hudson Motor Car Company, in 1954.

The new company was called AMC, or American Motors. A short time after its foundation, it had a new chief executive, George W. Romney.

Which leads you to his son, 2012 US presidential candidate, Mitt. Who said he didn't follow NASCAR racing closely. 'But I have some great friends who are NASCAR team owners.'

What was his other great man-of-the-people car quote? Click. 'I drive a Mustang and a Chevy pick-up truck. [Wife] Ann drives a couple of Cadillacs.'

Yes, a couple of them. And where *did* the Cadillac name come from? Ah, there it is … the impossibly pretentiously named French explorer Antoine Laumet de La Mothe, sieur de Cadillac.

He was the man who founded Detroit. Click. That's a sister city of Toyota, formerly Koromo city. Koromo was renamed in 1959 in honour of the importance of its main economic player, which has its Tsutsumi plant there. Toyota is a company that was never a big fan of forced induction, preferring the multi-valve approach. It wasn't until 1979, it says here, that Toyota finally produced a road car with a factory-fitted turbocharger. Which brings us vaguely back to where we started.

And, after wasting so much time trapped in hyperlink hell, has the damn motoring column been written? No, not a word of it.

46 Reasons you can't work on cars anymore

A cynic might say it's because if you could, you wouldn't take it back to the dealer.

The dealer, therefore, wouldn't be able to bill you hundreds or even thousands for recalibrating the bifurbicator, back-flushing the photon reservoir and decarbonising the sprugle-hitchen.

A less cynical person – presumably brought in from a different planet – might see it differently. They may argue, for safety's sake, that the average Joe shouldn't be chocking up the wheels in his carport, pulling out his Bunnings 250-piece socket set ($19.95) and trying to iron out a glitch in the electronic stability control system or radar cruise control.

Either way, a lack of serviceability is not a new complaint. Pliny the Elder probably wrote to his nephew in 78 AD: 'Just taken delivery of a new Maximus GTx chariot. Love the drinking-vessel holders, but appalled to discover that the entire underfloor assembly has just one part number.'

Pliny the Younger's reply, zipped straight to his uncle's inbox by a running slave, may have said: 'Know how you feel. Tried to buy a horseshoe yesterday and discovered you have to buy the whole horse. And they're sold only in blister packs of three.'

The power of positive tinkering.

Repair has been superseded by a newer model called Replace. Many of us look back warmly on the days of being able to buy every part down to the last washer and micro-gasket individually wrapped in tissue paper, of being up to our elbows in grease, of squeezing our arms down small, hot gaps and singeing our skin, of shredding knuckles to the bone when that bolt that *just won't move* suddenly … *ahhh*!

You can't beat the feeling of working on your own machine. That warm feeling of knowing that, although the procedure took all afternoon (rather than the planned twenty minutes), wrecked an expensive chrome body strip that you'll have to replace later, left an unsightly stain on the concrete and required a quick trip to the medical centre for a tetanus shot, you *did it yourself*.

Mind you, looking back warmly on those days is often preferable to reliving them. Particularly since the DIY bit was often required at short notice, on a narrow verge beside the road, in the rain, in a suit, while being sprayed by passing trucks.

It's interesting to be reminded of how much doing it yourself you had to do, even when things were going well. With, say, an early Holden there were daily, weekly and monthly checks. The engine oil had to be changed every 2000 miles (about 3200 km).

Owning a car back then was a big commitment. The service schedule for pre-WWII cars is even more frightening. The instruction manual from a 1920s example recommended that every single day you greased the valve rocker shaft and rockers, fan, front axle, steering lever bearing and rods, universal joint and spring shackles.

Every week you had to attend to the clutch shaft, foot-pedal bearings and brake rods, along with gear and brake lever bearings and shafts and associated linkages, steering wheel and throttle and spring bolts. The list continued with fortnightly, monthly and three-monthly filling, cleaning and greasing obligations.

By the 1980s and early 1990s service requirements had been reduced dramatically yet you could still maintain many cars entirely on your own.

Not so today. Not with modern integrated electronics and sealed systems. That said, although you can't work on today's cars, you usually don't need to. A modern Mercedes E-Class has 25,000-kilometre service intervals. That's nearly eight times that of an early Holden, despite the Merc being an immensely more complex and capable vehicle.

The cynic mentioned in the first paragraph might therefore wonder why the official service schedules of some legendarily well-built and reliable Japanese cars require them to be expensively looked at every 10,000 kilometres or six months (whichever comes first). Otherwise the sky will fall in and, more importantly, the warranty will be voided.

One can only assume they've begun using lower grade bifurbicators, photon reservoirs and sprugle-hitchens.

47 Multiple choice this time

1. Aside from being a forgettable Toyota, the Tercel is the male version of a hunting bird. But it's such a wimp that most hunters prefer the female of the species, which has also given its name to another car. What is the female called?
    (a) Falcon
    (b) Thunderbird
    (c) Budgie
    (d) Eagle

2. What Australian car answers to the following description? Body: fibreglass. Weight: 436 kilograms. Engine: Villiers two-stroke. Wheelbase: 1.88 metres. Other products built in same factory: power tools, car jacks, concrete-mixers.
    (a) Lightburn Zeta
    (b) Goggomobil Dart
    (c) Tilli Capton
    (d) Holden Kingswood

3. What's the connection between the Belgian playwright Maurice Maeterlinck and the World Land Speed Record?

    (a) Maeterlinck was the financial backer of Richard Noble's *Thrust 2* record-breaker

    (b) Malcolm Campbell's famous car was named after his play *The Bluebird*

    (c) His script *Breedlove: The Fastest Man on Wheels* was turned into a successful Broadway musical

    (d) Maeterlinck – also a counter-tenor singer and part-time race driver – died in 1926 trying to beat Henry Segrave's 245 km/h record

4. Kelvin, Farad and Henry are:

    (a) The given names of the Dodge Brothers

    (b) Units of the SI Metric system

    (c) The nicknames of the first three winners of the Bathurst 500

    (d) Three early General Motors brands

5. The Carioca was:

    (a) The name given to the first Lamborghini prototype

    (b) A streamlined Volvo car from the 1930s

    (c) A type of Swedish square-dancing that swept the world just after WWII

    (d) The car with which Preston Tucker hoped to follow his 'Torpedo'

6. Who achieved a speed of 655.73 km/h in 1963 to become the first man to claim the World Land Speed Record in a jet-powered car?
   (a) Gary Gabelich
   (b) Craig Breedlove
   (c) Graham Hill
   (d) Art Arfons

7. What car-centric song was supposedly written in a pink Edsel?
   (a) 'Little Deuce Coupe' by the Beach Boys
   (b) 'Beamer, Benz & Bentley' by Lloyd Banks with Juelz Santana
   (c) 'Faster' by George Harrison
   (d) 'Little Red Corvette' by Prince

8. More VW Beetles have been manufactured than any other single model. What is the total (approximately)?
   (a) 15.5 million
   (b) 18 million
   (c) 21.5 million
   (d) More than 25 million

9. Older Americans remember exactly where they were when they heard of President Kennedy's death. With Italians, it's more likely Enzo Ferrari. 'The Pope of the North' died in:
   (a) 1984
   (b) 1988
   (c) 1992
   (d) Bulgaria

10. Nissan's Pintara name came from:
    - (a) An Aboriginal word for beauty
    - (b) The name of a small town in rural Victoria
    - (c) An invented word with no literal meaning
    - (d) It's a Pintara, so who could possibly give a flying fluffy duck?

11. In 2011 a car fetched an auction record of US$16,390,000. This enormous – and highly publicised – sum was paid for:
    - (a) A Ferrari 250 Testa Rosso from 1957
    - (b) An Alfa Romeo racing car from the 1930s
    - (c) A 1971 Cadillac once owned by Elvis Presley
    - (d) A low-mileage Goggomobil Dart

12. What feat have Aussie race drivers Tony Gaze, Dave Walker and Paul England achieved?
    - (a) All have won the so-called Great Race at Bathurst
    - (b) All have competed in World Championship Formula One races
    - (c) All have been crowned World Speedway Champion
    - (d) All have survived high-speed accidents in Morris Marinas

NB Answers are on page 316.

48 What America's ultra-conservatives drive

To find out, one must turn to that font of knowledge known as Conservapedia.

Labelled 'The Trustworthy Encyclopedia', it was founded by Andrew Schlafly in 2006 to counter the pinko bias of that Maoist tract, Wikipedia.

Andrew is the son of high-profile American lawyer Phyllis Schlafly, known for opposing equal rights for women in the 1960s and pretty well every reform proposed thereafter.

What does Conservapedia say about motoring subjects? Here are some extracts, with typos and literals included. And, no, this is not a parody. There's plenty more at www.conservapedia.com.

Don't delay, visit today.

'**Toyota Motor Corporation** is a Japanese automobile manufacturing company founded in 1935. ... Toyota sells more hybrid electric vehicles than any other automobile manufacturer ... [these have]

The Trustworthy Encyclopedia

lower fuel efficiency than advertised, and having questionable battery life and cheap quality at for the vehicles expensive prices. They also are unsafe with danger of electrocution after an accident and they produce harmful electromagnetic radiation which can give you cancer.'

General Motors, we are told, 'was founded in 1908 by William C. Durant, and rose to become the world's leading auto manufacturers from the 1920s to 2008 … In 2006, over 9 million GM cars and trucks were sold. Since then a series of massive losses have brought GM into bankruptcy … GM is currently trying to find better ways to market to the homosexual community.'

Conservapedia's obsession with what consenting adults do in the privacy of their own godless, Marxist-Leninist dens of iniquity comes up again and again.

In the **Hybrid Car** entry we are told 'Hybrids are very popular with Hollywood celebrities, homosexuals and liberals', while the somewhat out-of-date **Mazda** entry includes such fair-minded and intensely relevant information as:

'Common complaints about Mazda vehicles are low power, high fuel consumption and terrible reliability. These days, their line up consists of econoboxes, the wankel powered RX-8 and the MX-5 which used to be called the Miata, this car has a known following in the homosexual community.'

Conservapedia is surprisingly upbeat – if not quite objective – in the **Ford** entry, saying the company 'did not request government aid in 2009 [and] now has to compete with the unfairly advantaged, mostly government-owned, GM and Fiat-owned Chrysler, both of which have had their past debts resolved … Despite this disadvantage, Ford continues to lead the world automotive market producing outstanding cars which destroy their European and Japanese competition.'

The entry for **Hummer** points out it was first a military vehicle but 'civilian interest grew after televised use in Desert Storm showed how

No party like a Tea Party. Thank goodness.

well the vehicles could handle off road terrain and how safe they were. The large size and poor fuel economy drew anger from liberals who want to dictate what people drive.'

True enough! Sopping wet, bleeding hearts don't realise **Global Warming** is a 'liberal hoax' and **Barack Hussein Obama** is 'almost certainly the first Muslim president of the United States'. Those dupes also think fossil fuels come from fossils. Take it away, Conservapedia:

> Mineral oils, such as petroleum, are obtained from geological sources. The latter is not formed by decayed matter … but instead during a *theobaric* process. This oil existed in pristine state before the Flood, and moved during the Flood into the reservoirs where Noah emerged from the Ark, and where we now find it. Consequently much of the oil is found in the Middle East …

What the hell, you ask, is a theobaric process? Follow the Conservapedia footnote, dummy!: '**Theobaric** (Gk., *theo-*, God; *bar*, weighty) means "made by God". This word was recently coined by John D. Matthews.'

Ah, now it's all clear. Imagine what we could come to believe if we used an untrustworthy encyclopaedia!

49 Car theft, from go to woe

The thieving of cars is a billion-dollar industry that affects us all (in increased insurance rates, at the very least). So it seems likely someone would have produced a social history of the phenomenon.

Alas, there are no obvious tomes, despite there being histories of the traffic accident, even one on the automobile-as-explosive device (Mike Davis's book *Buda's Wagon: A Brief History of the Car Bomb*).

There are, of course, books and learned papers on the legal side of car theft, and strategies for preventing it happening to you. There are publications too about computer games that glamorise it.

These include the delightfully named *GTA-ology – What I Need to Know in Life I Learned from Playing Grand Theft Auto*. Yes, honestly. Author Ty Liquido promises that you'll 'Explore ways to turn your life into a GTA-styled, MISSION GALORE adventure'. Strangely, some of us have other plans.

So when did car stealing begin? A typically America-centric web reference suggests the *Des Moines Tribune* reported the first case of auto theft in the US. It happened in 1905, 'nine years after the first automobile theft in the world, in France'.

More rifling around produced equally unsourced, and possibly just as dodgy, information on that 1896 French theft. It occurred in Paris when a mechanic nicked a Peugeot that Baron de Zuylen de Nyevelt had put in the workshop for repairs.

Baron who? Turns out the Dutch-born car enthusiast was the first President of the FIA, the international motoring body set up to ensure that, some time in the distant future, Ferrari would be allowed to use a different rulebook to everyone else in Formula One.

Details on the second-ever car theft are harder to find, though further trawling turned up some more easily cross-referenced material about carjacking. It seems it was also pioneered in France, and as early as 1912.

Anarchists stopped a De Dion south of Paris and shot the driver. They used the purloined car to rob a bank, successfully escaping despite having two policemen hot on their exhaust pipes. It may have been significant that one was on a horse, the other madly pedalling a bicycle.

The New York Times' archives turn up an interesting piece from 1922, headlined 'First Stolen Rolls-Royce.' It explains how the said

Roller, worth $16,000 and the property of one Howard Friend (his full address is given), was reported missing shortly after 'two o'clock yesterday morning'.

The owner had parked it near Eighty-ninth Street 'while he visited friends'. A tabloid publication would have asked the important questions, such as exactly what 'friends' Howard was visiting at that hour. It would have also added some unattributed quotes from a 'close family friend' explaining that Howie's marriage was in the toilet because of his penchant for mysterious late night trysts.

Flashes Stolen Car Warning

THE latest development in the war against automobile thieves is an electric appliance that flashes out the word "stolen" as soon as a thief attempts to turn on the ignition switch. The secret lies in a tiny locked box on the back of the dashboard. Connection is made with the ignition system, and unless the driver of the car adjusts the mechanism the letters blaze out.

Thieves can't go far with car equipped as shown.

The *NYT*, however, was content to merely state that the car was 'recovered by Detectives Styme, Kane and Reilley of the Automobile Squad some twelve hours later … abandoned on Amsterdam Avenue near Eighty-first Street'. What an innocent age, when you could go out late at night in your Rolls-Royce to engage in moral turpitude without the media giving you a hard time. And you could confidently assume that the Automobile Squad was on your side.

How things change.

50 For auction: 1964 Tortellini Superleggera GT

Presented here is a superb example of the Tortellini Superleggera GT, the much sought-after one-door coupe built by ex-Ferrari engineer Guido Tortellini and his brother Luigi during the early 1960s.

Famed for its motor sport participation, and for its unusual V13 engine, the Tortellini marque more than deserved its reputation as 'the Ferrari with more'. Collectors will note this particular Superleggera GT is an ultra-rare Omologato 54-C3a version with weight-saving *papier mâché* body panels and cellophane windows instead of glass.

It comes with the matching Scuderia Tortellini fuel-trailer. This so successfully allowed it to avoid pit-stops during longer races, though caused jack-knifing and the subsequent burning down of two grandstands at the Grand Hotel Hairpin during Tortellini's one Monaco GP appearance in 1962.

The Superleggera GT's single 'budgie-wing door' passed into supercar legend, particularly after Enrico Bigamotori, the Tortellini driver who achieved a top ten class finish in the 1961 Le Mans 24 Hour, ended up circulating for another 48 hours due to a jammed throttle and a problem with the elaborate door handle arrangements.

Although built primarily for racing, this example comes with conditional

Australian registration that allows it to be used on private roads that are at least 1500 metres from any public building or house of worship.

Our auction house's Director of Collector Cars, Simon Lastard, says: 'This fine example with its strong claims of authenticity will please the most fastidious buyer. It used as its starting point a car that was still unfinished when production stopped in 1964 due to the factory, in the western suburbs of Modena, being struck by a meteor.

'Although only the grille and light assembly were pulled from the crater, all other work was completed entirely in the spirit of the original under the guidance, and in the lounge room, of Roberto Favoria, who worked in the staff canteen during the original production run.'

The car pictured here is sold 'as is' with no further guarantees, and is available for inspection between 1 p.m. and 1.10 p.m. from the other side of a very wide river.

This example was sold by Favoria as a new car to an Indian buyer in 1969 who, when he peeled off the Ferrari stickers and discovered it was a Tortellini, apparently on-sold it to a Welsh company that briefly used the thirteen-cylinder engine (fed by a row of 7.5 Dellorto carburettors) to pump water out of its coal mines.

It was only after one of the pit engineers realised the historic significance of the V13 that it was reunited with the body shell – by then badly deteriorated – and sold to Glyn Glynn-Glynnn, the famed Pontypool racing driver.

Its bodywork is still finished in the Corsa Marrone (Welsh Racing Brown) in which it finished its last race, on a street circuit in a Pembrokeshire mining valley in 2001. It has travelled only 500 kilometres since a superb ground-up restoration.

This included a new replica chassis, a replacement engine block and internals, a superb interior crafted from the same type of cows as supplied the original leather and a new body using only high-end broadsheet newspapers.

A hand-built, all-aluminium version of the famous nine-speed Tortellini manual gearbox, purchased over the Internet from the QingPing company in Guizhou, is also included.

This car's chassis and engine numbers match, in that neither is legible, and it comes with a fine provenance including a handwritten note from the original buyer in his native language of Meiteilon (Rongmei dialect). Translation is the bidder's responsibility.

Since its restoration, this car has been meticulously maintained with a full engine and gearbox rebuild after each use, as recommended in the original owner's handbook.

In terms of price guidance, Lastard says: 'We confidently predict a bid of $485,500, though it is entirely possible someone who doesn't work for our auction house will offer even more.'

51 A short treatise on superhero transport

The most famous superhero conveyance of all is the Batmobile, notwithstanding the deep philosophical question of whether its owner is really a superhero.

What exactly are Batman's special powers? Could he be just a normal man with a fancy costume, a good tool kit and novel ideas about how he should be spending his downtime?

His original car, from the 1939 comic book, was fairly subdued. The fins and bat logos were added progressively and by the 1960s television series the 'Batmobile' was looking like a Mardi-Gras float.

The 1966 movie gave us a motorcycle with a low-slung, high-camp, self-propelled sidecar for the Boy Wonder.

In recent films, Bat-vehicles have assumed a more noir look. Batman has driven not only a Batmobile but also a military-based 'Tumbler' that spits out a Batpod. The Batpod is a very uncomfortable, machine gun-equipped motorcycle, steered with the shoulders.

Superman is unquestionably a superhero. He doesn't need a young and impeccably coiffured sidekick, for a start. That might be why he doesn't need a car, either. Who'd drive a machine if they could fly without one?

All together now: nana-nana-nana-na Batman! Batman!

Like many of these guys, though, Superman has an everyday persona, and that persona needs to get around without revealing any super powers.

In the 1950s television series starring George Reeves, Clark Kent drove a 1953 Nash-Healey. This Nash-Kelvinator Corporation roadster predated the Corvette and was hailed as the first American sports car of the post-WWII era.

It was actually an amalgam of English, Italian and American parts – and an odd choice for someone wanting to deflect attention.

Also, it was never explained how a mild-mannered reporter could afford a car costing twice that of the Chevy competitor. Was Superman doing freelance security work on weekends, or giving paid tip-offs to *The News of the World*?

Another category of superhero that shouldn't need a car is the type that can swing on a web. Yet Spiderman drove an All Terrain Vehicle with a 'pollution free' engine in a comic book. Described as the Spidermobile, it looked like a shortened Meyers Manx dune buggy with a web-pattern paint job.

The first word that came to mind was 'unnecessary'. The second was lame. It ended up in the Hudson River, where it probably belonged.

In the 1967 television show, 'Captain Scarlet and the Mysterons', the marionette star drove an oddly proportioned, four-wheel drive, '195 mph', wedge-nosed Patrol. A gas turbine engine was in the back; the brakes were electromagnetic. It also had airbags, which was odd since Captain Scarlet was indestructible.

Wonderwoman had an invisible jet, which saved on special effects.

The Green Hornet's associate, Kato, drove their Black Beauty. In the 1940s movie serial, this '200 mph' car was a tarted-up 1937 Lincoln-Zephyr, which stretched credibility just a little.

In later TV and film renditions, including the 2011 movie, it was a sixties-style American land yacht, which stretched it even further. Although fitted with discreet guns and other armoury, this Chrysler Imperial-based vehicle lacked the elegance of, say, superspy James Bond's similarly equipped Aston-Martin DB5.

A website called Superhero Law looks at masked crime-fighting from a legal perspective. Yes, really. It points out that not only are most super-vehicles unregistered, they are almost certainly uninsured. A valid policy would require the superhero's real name and address, and that simply isn't going to be provided.

Superheros have boats that fail to display visible identification numbers and none seek Federal Aviation Administration approval for their flying machines, nor do they file flight paths.

Superhero Law lists legal problems with super-vehicle exhausts, emissions, window tinting and more. Depending on your point of view, this is a fascinating perspective, or positive proof that some people have way too much time on their hands.

Parody superheros need vehicles too: Mr Incredible's Incredobile looked somewhat 1960s Italian, and was equipped with the *de rigueur* guns and ejector seat. Batfink's getabout was more modest: a pink VW Beetle with rear wings (rather than fins). It was known as the Battilac.

Why stop at superheroes? Here are some other cars that are pure fiction:

Powell 'Homer' – An everyman's car designed by Homer Simpson, following the discovery that his lost half-brother, Herb Powell, owned his own major automobile company. Homer let his design muse run free, giving his car twin dome cockpits, three horns, tailfins and an exhaust note that sounded like 'the world is coming to an end'. Homer's handiwork sent Powell Motors broke, but Bart thought it was cool.

Fiasco – The protagonist of Martin Amis's novel *Money*, the narcissistically named John Self drove a Fiasco sports car. The author wrote himself into the book as a character too, at the wheel of an Iago 666. Other cars mentioned were the Alibi, the Farrago, the Hyena and the luxury Autocrat.

Nike ONE – An alternative energy open-wheeler created for the computer game Gran Turismo 4. It supposedly uses HEP Drive, which stands for Human Energy Potential. This gathers its power from a Nike Spark Suit and stores it in the batteries of the driver's shoes. Yes, really. No doubt if this '370 km/h' vehicle ever comes to market, it will be ludicrously overpriced and built in a Third World crèche.

Turbo Terrific – A dragster with a rather extreme front overhang driven by Peter Perfect in the animated television series *The Wacky Races*. Love interest Penelope Pitstop drove the Compact Pussycat while Dick Dastardly, the requisite Snidely Whiplash-type character, drove the Mean Machine, along with his dog Muttley.

Spinner – Flying cars are a mainstay of science fiction. Those in the dystopian film *Blade Runner* (1982) were known as 'Spinners,' and seemed to be in the hands only of police and ultra-rich people. Spinners could drive on land, take off vertically, hover and do everything else you'd expect a car to be capable of by 2019, when the film was set.

Yamura – The Japanese Formula One team in *Grand Prix*, the 1966 John Frankenheimer film. It was blatantly based on Honda with the

Captain Scarlet's Patrol.

inscrutable team principal, Izo Yamura, spending a lot of screen time being inscrutable.

Vaillante – Another fictitious F1 team, this one existing entirely within a comic book – sorry, graphic novel. It was the marque raced by Michel Vaillante, famed fictional French driver. Vaillante produced a few road cars too. Matra, it seems, was the model.

Betsy – Named after the boss's daughter, the radical new Betsy was supposed to save the Hardeman car company. As befitting the source – a Harold Robbins paperback – it was designed by a womanising racing driver. Although built in Detroit in the 1970s, the Betsy was fuel efficient, clean running and ultra-durable, reinforcing the extent of the fiction. Laurence Olivier was somehow persuaded to participate in the 1978 film (also called *The Betsy*). The car was played by a fairly crudely modified Lancia coupe, supposedly powered by a turbine engine.

Light Runner – Light cycles are those luminous two-wheel creations that race though the Tron universe. The *Tron Legacy* film introduced a fifth-generation Light Runner so cool a few street-legal replicas were made (though none were quite as quick as the movie incarnation, nor ran on pure liquid energy).

NMC Hawk – Not to be confused with the Studebaker Hawk, this was built by National Motors Corporation in the television series of the Arthur Hailey novel *Wheels* (the car was called the Orion in the book). Hailey spat out heavily researched, kazillion-selling airport reads (including, fittingly, *Airport*) and Ford Motor Company was the model for his fictitious car company. The youth-oriented Hawk was conceived by NMC's boss, Rock Hudson (in the television series, at least). It had gullwing doors. And was pug ugly.

52 What happened to the Fabulous McPhibbys?

The McPhibby brothers were titans of Australian motor sport who came to prominence in the 1970s, though the story goes back much further.

Peter, Dick and Mark were the racing sons of Stanley 'Squibby' McPhibby, who won the 1954 Australian Grand Prix in a stolen Ford Customline, en route to a bank job.

While Stanley served time for exceeding the speed limit by more than 15 mph – that was of the most interest to police – the boys made the most of their time on the family's idyllic hidden Queensland farm, with its generous supply of late-model cars without ignition barrels.

The brothers learned to drive fast, particularly when police helicopters swooped above. As engineers they were self-taught, trim and terrific.

Their eventual building of a 28-kilometre, 170-corner track on the farm, known locally as the Northbundabergring, helped sharpen their driving and car preparation skills.

Early victories on public circuits came in homemade cars, including the notoriously difficult-to-drive 'McPhibby Special' with its De Soto running gear and unusual house-brick construction. This Special was later to be fitted with an eleven-cylinder engine made by welding a Daihatsu straight three across the front of a Ford Flathead V8. It continued to win races, but vibrated so much it shook out young Mark's teeth.

The term 'The Fabulous McPhibbys' came about at this time, when the boys placed first, second and third in the Brisbane 300 street race. All three brothers lapped every other competitor – and each other – before staging the most confusing form-finish in motor sport history.

Dick, although famously slow out of the car, proved spritely around Bathurst once Team McPhibby fitted a map to the dashboard that helped him find his way. He could also deliver semi-witty, pre-written lines, earning a reputation as laconic, a word he could never find in the dictionary.

Mark, born with a more serviceable brain but without a personality, had an extraordinary post-race ability to reel off the names of sponsors and commercial partners until everyone in the audience was comatose.

Peter was the charismatic head of the operation, as well as the most successful driver.

By 1980 the brothers were building hot versions of the last series Valiant, though neither the slogan 'Body by Mitsubishi Australia but based on the original Chrysler one, Soul by McPhibby,' nor the vehicle itself – with two Hemi straight sixes side-by-side under that wide CM series bonnet – ever quite caught the popular imagination.

When Peter invented a small firewall-mounted device said to wirelessly harness the power of reiki, yoga, cold fusion and napalm, it led not only to an acrimonious break with Mitsubishi, it also caused the sectioning off of whole Adelaide suburbs, some of which are still considered no-go areas.

It seems remarkable now to reflect that no McPhibby ever lost a motor race during the entire 1980s or early 1990s, except to another person with the same surname.

Some connected this to the instalment of Stanley 'Squibby' McPhibby as team manager. He, and his associate Lefty, took a dim view of anyone overtaking his boys – or his wife Gladys. She won two rounds of the Australian Touring Car Championship in 1986 in the family four-wheel drive with its horse float still hitched.

Others say such a view is disingenuous, except Dick, who couldn't find that word in the dictionary either.

The family's retirement, en masse, in 1995 brought the era to a sudden close, though not before Peter switched cars twice at Bathurst and became the only driver ever to finish first, second and third.

The Fabulous McPhibbys. Their like will not be seen again.

53 What language are brochures written in?

A brochure, indeed all marketing material, is written in an ancient patois still spoken as a first language in small pockets of the globe. Such as Fantasyland.

'The new Civic Type R is even hotter,' screams one clarion call for a new Honda, but two lines further down we learn, 'It's as cool to look at as it is to drive.'

Nissan's 370 Z car promises not extreme and unpredictable temperature variations, but 'a 370-degrees shift'. Even for those of us lacking much interest in geometry, such a shift would appear to bring us very close to where we started. Yeah, I'd pay a premium for that.

What about something really dull but competent – how do the guff writers get around that?

'In the search for perfection,' the Toyota people tell us, 'no stone was left unturned by Camry's designers.'

It's built like that because of something they found under a rock? And, hang on, if the Camry is perfect, why are there dearer (or indeed other) vehicles in the range?

The FPV F6 (a fancy name for a Ford Falcon fed too much red cordial) is presented as 'one perfectly engineered driving machine'. Nope, no hyperbole there either.

Maserati's Quattroporte has, apparently, 'prodigious power, inspirational handling and sumptuous luxury [providing] the fortunate few with an unparalleled driving experience'. Exactly what is an unparalleled driving experience? Does the Quattroporte never do the same thing twice, or perhaps refuse to follow the white lines on the side of the road? And what does the handling inspire drivers to do?

It can't be easy, though. The advertising standards code keeps forcing performance carmakers to find new ways of being irresponsible without being irresponsible. You are simply not allowed to say fast cars are fun, even if you are selling fast cars. And even if, as we all know, fast cars are fun.

There are other impediments. Holden has argued the Commodore Sportwagon is better in every way than a soft-roader 4WD. This has required readers to overlook that the same company also flogs a soft-roader – for which it claims just as many advantages.

While talking about Holden language, there's the term 'leather-appointed seating'. McDonald's would be proud of that one.

'All the leather we use is 100 per cent leather.'

'Yes but how much of it do you use?'

'You're not listening to me, boy. All our leather is 100 per cent leather. Leather doesn't come any more leathery than that.'

Marketing blather doesn't only tell us something about the people who wrote it. It usually tells us the type of customers being sought. Look at the billboard containing a photo of a Harley-Davidson and the slogan '331 screws included'.

Yep, even the sad, dim, desperado is considered a targetable demographic if you can find the right words to inspire him or her to open the wallet. (In this case, it's definitely a 'him'; who else would spend some tens of thousands of dollars in the expectation a sports tractor would produce results like that?)

A favourite press release opens with: 'South Korea has been doing more than scanning the northern horizon for missiles in recent months: it's been busy preparing for the launch of its own missiles.'

Now some may question the wisdom of linking your products to technologically suss and horribly erratic weapons that are scaring the crap out of much of the world. But Hyosung thought it was a good way to tell us that its motorcycles 'now feature fuel-injection across the entire 250 cc and 650 cc V-twin 2010 model range'.

That would be the entire range of some of the company's models then.

The sales brochure for the Ferrari 458 Italia could otherwise be described as a large-format, high-gloss hardback book. It's such an expensive publication, you have to be pretty serious about buying a half-million-dollar car before they'll give you a copy. That, or a freeloading journalist.

Having a massive budget for your brochure is helped further if you are pitching a photogenic car. After turning the silver endpapers of the 458 effort, the reader will find the next nine pages featuring nothing but dazzling shots of that dazzling bodywork.

Then there's more silver paper, a prancing horse logo and those immortal opening words: *'Alla base di tutto, nel mondo, c'è il sogno.'* This is Italian for 'We could be talking any drivel, and it wouldn't matter because here's another photo of a bright red, lust-bucket 458'.

The English script underneath confirms it truly is drivel: 'Dreams drive all human activity. They are the engine of history, our passport to the future.' But no matter, here are some pictures of historic Ferraris. And more silvery paper, and schematics of dry sump V8s with multi-coloured charts showing the power and torque, and close-ups of the brakes, lights, steering wheel and exhaust pipes in macro, salacious detail. It might as well say 'come on, you know you want it'. Having the brochure

in two languages, even if it says little in either, adds to the exotic appeal. The cosmetic industry puts French words on anything expensive and Italian is clearly the best foreign language for an exotic car.

The last page of the Ferrari brochure is a full-page photo of a yellow 458 driving into the sunset, probably with a now hocked-to-the-hilt brochure reader behind the wheel.

54 Origins of the traffic jam

The phenomenon goes back to Roman times, at the very least. Archaeologists have found evidence of gridlock in Pompeii and elsewhere.

In Ancient Rome itself, the traffic grew so intense that J. Caesar declared a daytime ban on carts and chariots.

Among the few exceptions to this ban, according to Tom Vanderbilt's 2008 book *Traffic*, were those vehicles transporting construction materials for temples and great public works.

Vanderbilt didn't mention though that politicians and people with consular plates probably continued to do as they damn well pleased.

The original Appian Way – Rome's great road – passed through the Italian city of Terracina, passing over the Monte Sant'Angelo along the way so that travellers could pop into the temple of Jupiter Anxur.

As a result, the steep and narrow road was almost permanently clogged by temple-goers, rubberneckers and other road hogs. It was probably also lined with signs saying 'Centurions are now targeting speeding'.

Work began on a new side road from about 184 BC. Squeezed between mountain and sea, it enabled travellers to give the temple the flick. Yes, it was the world's first bypass.

For the next couple of thousand years, traffic was so light that most places didn't need bypasses. Heck, they didn't even need an agreement on which side of the road one had to drive, ride or walk.

Standstills only really happened on bridges, near major public monuments or during wars. The rise of mega-cities, however, enabled them to become part of everyday life.

In 1888 New York's *The Sun* newspaper ran the headline 'Traffic Jammed Streets', though it was another couple of decades before the words 'traffic' and 'jam' were regularly slammed together.

Since it received its name, every country in the world has been trying to perfect the 'traffic jam'. A record 100-kilometre jam was, like most other things you see nowadays, made in China. It happened in August 2010 when an unusually large number of heavy trucks coincided with a road maintenance program on a road rather laughingly called National Expressway 110.

It didn't unhappen for eleven whole days, providing a bonanza for roadside vendors.

Although the longest in duration, the Chinese logjam wasn't the longest in, er, longness. The French created a 176-kilometre car park stretching from Lyon towards Paris in 1980. It was the result of bad weather and an influx of ski-field traffic.

Just under ten years later, a numerical record was set when an estimated 18 million cars were wedged together around the East–West German border. Something to do with a wall coming down.

Worse by the minute: Beijing traffic.

Cyclones, hurricanes, bushfires and earthquakes tend to cause major jams. But for sheer everyday misery, *TIME* magazine declares that traffic jams in São Paulo, Brazil, are without equal.

Ayrton Senna, who honed his technique there, once said, 'If you fail to go for a gap that exists, you are no longer a racing driver.' You probably aren't a São Paulo commuter either.

If ranked for entertainment, the best traffic jam could well be the one in *The Italian Job* (the original film from 1969; accept no substitutes). The plot revolved around a gold heist by British crims. They facilitated their getaway by tampering with Turin's computerised traffic management system, thereby bringing almost all vehicles – except three Minis – to a standstill.

Although there was plenty of Hollywood in the stunts (they went through at least ten Minis), the massive blockages captured on camera were real. Reports as to how they were created range from suggestions the Italian mafia closed down the streets to help film-makers (and perhaps obtain money for jam!), to reports that Turinians were invited to participate in the world's biggest traffic jam and proved more than willing.

Another theory: film-makers simply parked their vans in strategic locations and filmed the results. Cheap but effective.

TECHNICALITIES
55 Are these good ideas?

Good ideas are only considered good because they stand out from the rest. So let's use this opportunity to focus on 'the rest'.

Well, why not? After all, anyone who ignores the lessons of history is bound to repeat them. In this noble search for *in*excellence, we've rescued a few truly daft vehicles from the dust of the archives.

The sQuba – Swiss car maker Rinspeed has built some of the downright oddest machines ever to grace the halls of the world's motor shows. Most of them are, mercifully, 'one-offs', but the sQuba may not be.

When presented at the 2008 Geneva Car show it was described as 'the world's first real submersible car'. This missed the point that any

The sQuba

Flinkel Fluff GT.

car can be submerged – as car thieves and bad drivers have shown through the years. It was more a matter of the sQuba being able to 'unsubmerge' under its own power.

The sQuba is courageously built around a Lotus Elise, a vehicle that lets in water even when on the road. Power is entirely electric, with rechargeable lithium-ion batteries hidden in the composite and aluminium bodywork. According to the guff, the vehicle can 'perform a submerged stabile flight at a depth of 10 meters'.

The 'automarine' (or 'submobile') was the brainchild of Rinspeed boss Frank M. Rinderknecht, a James Bond enthusiast with a particular liking for *The Spy Who Loved Me*. In that 1977 film Roger Moore's Lotus Esprit was driven into the sea, where it immediately, miraculously converted into a submarine.

Rinderknecht said: 'For three decades I have tried to imagine how it might be possible to build a car that can fly under water. Now we have made this dream come true.'

Built at a claimed cost of $1.5 million, Rinspeed reckons the sQuba (a) really works and (b) will soon go into production. We'll believe it when one drives down a boat ramp and we don't see it.

Flinkel Fluff GT – The whole idea of the DIY car seems to have lost favour in recent years. Looking at this Australian example from 1982, it's hard to see why. After all, it doesn't look like comfort, safety or refinement have been compromised in any way.

Built by Joe Flinkier, it was known as the Flinkel Fluff GT and was in its day claimed as the smallest registered car in Australia. The choice of name suggests that if Joe had an eye for marketing, it was closed at the time.

GM Puma – A joint venture with Segway, makers of the amazing gyroscopically stabilised personal mobility platform, this half-arsed GM concept was shown at the 2009 New York Motor Show. Why half-arsed? It

GM Puma.

Tang Hua Book of Songs.

wasn't even finished (hence the lack of bodywork; the finished car was shown as a 'rendering'). Thanks to Segway technology, the PUMA is self-righting despite having its two road wheels side by side. It's shorter than a motorcycle. As for production, we'll believe it when PUMAs are on display at thousands of dealerships. And even then we'll be suspicious.

Tang Hua – There is a theory that China will slay the world in the electric car market, thanks partly to its exploiting of a near-monopoly on a whole lot of rare and useful minerals. In the meantime, the battery-powered Tang Hua Book of Songs (no kidding), shown by the catchily named Beijing Li Shi Guang Ming Auto Design Co. in 2008, looks like it benefits from design input from Pixar.

56 The fascinating Devrim

The Devrim is a car, and a famous one, albeit only in Turkey. And it's probably famous there mainly for making one of the most embarrassing product debuts in automotive history.

Which we'll come to shortly.

Well, come on … a bloke should be allowed a few blatant journalistic hooks if he's trying to make people interested in an obscure Turkish sedan.

On its fiftieth anniversary, the unusual gestation of the Devrim became the subject of a feature film. This was despite only four examples ever being made and despite, well, that embarrassing unveiling. Which we'll come to shortly.

The only other car that springs to mind as inspiring a 'making of' feature film is the 1948 Tucker, later known as the Torpedo. The Tucker, of which about fifty-eight were made, was considered Hollywood material because it had a radical design and a charismatic man behind it who managed to spin the story that he was going to smash Detroit.

When he didn't, he spun the story that Detroit's skulduggery had smashed him.

And the Devrim? The story started when Turkey had a general election – which is to say, an election involving only generals – and Cemal Gürsel was installed as president.

The Devrim in all its glory.

General Gürsel decided it would be good for morale if Turkey designed and produced a car all of its own – ideally within four months, in time for the 1961 Republic Day celebrations.

Despite the ludicrous time frame, only about two dozen engineers were drafted into the project. They had limited resources and even more limited experience. Some of them had never driven a car, let alone designed or engineered one, so didn't necessarily know quite what they were trying to achieve.

Although said to be thwarted at every point by bureaucracy, they worked around the clock to pull apart any cars they could get their hands on, then reverse engineer all they'd learned into a prototype sedan known as the Devrim. That's Turkish for 'revolution'. The Devrim looked vaguely like a small piece of late-fifties Americana and was powered by a 2-litre engine developing about 38 kW. Two of the four examples (the two closest to being finished) were put on the train to Ankara for the celebrations, but even they weren't that close to being finished. One was reputedly painted en route.

There hadn't been time to make engineering drawings either, meaning that series production was going to be difficult.

Still, in front of a large and enthusiastic crowd, the president stepped into the new Turkish sedan outside the National Parliament. A dream was about to be realised. Or not.

One hundred metres later the car spluttered to a halt, and the rather embarrassed president jumped out, presumably muttering the Turkish word for 'bugger'.

He climbed into the second car and, although that went further, the damage was done. Devrim jokes circulated and the president himself threw in a few jibes for good measure.

The problem was simple and minor: in the rush, the first car hadn't been fuelled. General G is quoted (in one translation) as saying: 'The team developed the automobile with Western mind, however forgot to supply the fuel with Eastern mind.'

The event spelled the end of the Devrim, so at least the lack of engineering drawings no longer mattered.

In concept, the Devrim was nothing new. The Holden and the VW Beetle (pre-war and post-war versions) are among many cars pushed along by governments with at least one eye on nation-boosting. Sadly, the Devrim ended up more a nation-reducing exercise.

In 2009 Turkish director Tolga Ornek told the story in *Chariots of Revolution* (or *Devrim Arabalari*). Some may worry about a film set mostly inside the Eskisehir Train and Locomotive Manufacturing Plant of State Railroad Directorate, but *Chariots of Revolution* earned rave reviews in its homeland.

57 The toughest driving of all

No question about it. Anyone who has competed in the daily 9.15 a.m. Grand Prix will know that desert raids, ice racing and rallying through tall forests just aren't in the same league.

As we all know, school-running is one branch of motor sport where the lower formula – Primary – is even tougher and more fiercely fought than the premier class, High.

There I was just the other day, surrounded by screaming engines, the lights about to change, the battle imminent.

The lead was mine for a short while heading towards the parked cars on the left. But suddenly it was like having Sebastian Vettel to

one side and Fernando Alonso to the other. And if dealing with these barge-masters wasn't enough, the two team managers in my own back seat were giving contrary instructions.

A man in a suit, driving a 4WD with roo-bar (he must have been dropping off his kids en route to his job in the Pilbara), rounded me up on the outside.

A woman stuck her nose out from a side street. The placement of her machine made it clear she believed she was already on the racing line and that I should yield; that the corner coming up before the intersection and the 40 km/h zone was hers by rights.

I lifted, looked to the left and right, crested the hill, willed the front end to sit and grip, as I lined up the zebra crossing and the man with the lollypop sign.

I swerved left then right to avoid the new entrants who must have started in the pit lane. Or, more likely, the bus lane. They were arriving from every direction, apparently without a single functioning blinker between them.

Except, of course, when they were using all four blinkers – the *park anywhere lights* – to indicate a right-left-swerving three-point ramming manoeuvre prior to a complete stop for a chat in the middle of the narrow road next to the double yellow lines. Well, when else does one get a chance to talk to Emma's mother?

There are other major differences between these drivers and those in most forms of motor sport. Many school-runners, including those at the front of the pack, are able to talk on the phone during a braking duel, often while also passing a bottle of something to the riding mechanic in the booster seat in the rear.

Some can do all of the above while waving at that woman jaywalking across the road with her straggly two sons, and while simultaneously inspecting and critically evaluating the artwork that Imogen in the front seat did before class.

Some may be annoyed at this type: the sort who would nominate driving as the biggest distraction they have to face when behind the wheel. But think of how much bravery is involved (or stupidity, no, I'm sure it's bravery). And think how much assembled talent makes it to the grid each day, with a fiery, aggressive, never-say-back-off determination.

In what other form of the sport are competitors courageous enough to speed up 25 per cent when it's raining? To unclick their seatbelts well before the finish line? To disregard pit boards when the messages don't suit them?

Which other motor sport practitioners have no compunction about sticking one, two or all four wheels into spectator areas if it yields an advantage? Or, if they can't nose in front, will double-park then throw open their doors to catch – or at the very least intimidate – passing competitors?

Yes, the daily Grand Prix de Primary can be cage fighting without the decorum.

How do we as a nation harness this rare blend of skill and gamesmanship? Where's the development plan for these drivers to advance to the better-paying formulae and eventually demonstrate to those show-pony F1 drivers what true grit is all about?

Where is the annual Parent to Europe scholarship?

58 A masterpiece to some

OK, whether it is or isn't a masterpiece depends on how you look at it. And if you do so with your eyes open, you may decide no.

Talking here about *Running on Empty*, an Ozploitation, carsploitation, Deborah-Conway-with-her-top-offsploitation film from 1982.

For all its faults – there's about eighty-eight minutes of them if you count the credits – it's fun in parts, stars what is claimed as a genuine Falcon GT-HO Phase III, and has a solid fan-base, even all these years later.

The plot is production-line stuff: guy has hot car, becomes involved in speed racing, gets the girl, loses the girl, wins the race, loses the race, gets heavied by heavies, etc.

Curiously, most of the characters look more like overly preened, ultra-fashion-conscious members of the Duran Duran fan club than knife-wielding outsiders. In real life, most 1980s street racers were more like journalist Steve Rushin's classic description of NASCAR fans: 'tattooed, shirtless, sewer-mouthed drunks … and their husbands.'

Still, this is Hollywood. Or desperately wants to be. But check those hairstyles: proof that Australia was once a mulletocracy.

The police – always the same two (Grahame Bond and Penne Hackforth-Jones) – look straight from *The Rocky Horror Show*. The racing is most interesting when a truck pulls out in front of the cars, or the bad loser decides to deliberately crash and turn his car into an instant, unconvincing fireball. This happens not once, but twice.

Many of the cars were apparently prime examples on loan from enthusiasts. That's why they suddenly turn into something more modest just before their automotive Armageddon (the Hoey is shunted and rebuilt by the characters three times).

Film-makers can't fool geeks in this day and age. 'In the first drag race of the movie,' says one blogger, 'Fox is racing a yellow Holden Monaro. During the burnout the Monaro sounds like a V8 when [it] crashes, the hood flies off and a six-cylinder engine is clearly visible.'

Another points out that a 1969 HT Monaro turns into a 1968 HK ('note the tail-lights'). When a supposedly manual Falcon is loaded on to the truck, a glimpse of the underside shows it's an auto. I couldn't quite build up the enthusiasm for slow-moing, though many of the switches are obvious at full speed.

At one stage the HO (either the real one, or one of the stand-ins) gets an amazing amount of air over a crest.

The dialogue is mostly gruesome. HO owner Mike (Terry Serio) loves cars 'because maybe soon there won't be any'. He's not quite James Dean when he says, 'Being free just scares some people shitless, doesn't it?'

Julie (Deborah Conway) is given mostly twaddle to talk, but eventually makes a big feministy speech. Mike responds by pushing her into a fridge and saying, 'This is equal rights for women.' The logic of this retort did escape me …

There are some interesting scenes of 'old' Sydney, including the then-barren Hickson Road in The Rocks, a real street-racing venue. When the characters go bush, you can see the *Mad Max* influence (the original *MM* had been made three years earlier).

One of *Running on Empty*'s more surreal characters is a blind mechanic named Rebel (Max Cullen), who blasts up and down the deserted highway in the dark in his blown 57 Chev coupe.

Rebel offers to nitrous-inject Mike's car so he can win the do-or-die duel. All today's viewer can think is 'don't touch a thing, you'll destroy its value. If you want to fix something, start with the haircuts.'

The nostalgia isn't just with the cars. At one stage Mike and his sidekick Tony look for a job in a newspaper. It's literally packed with classified advertisements. Fancy that.

59 How do you announce nothing?

Attention all media: The 2013 model Cistern 30P is now available in new car showrooms across the country, weeks ahead of the originally scheduled launch.

The newcomer brings changes that make the highly popular family sedan more appealing than ever, and which are certain to cement its place in the new vehicle sales charts.*

Subtlety has been the main theme with the revisions, yet they thoroughly refresh the model from its stylish nose to its assertive tail.

Enthusiasts will delight in the fact that the award-winning Cistern designers have chosen not to tamper with the classy exterior lines, opting instead for delicate and restrained touches that draw out the expressive character of the vehicle.

These include a dark highlight strip above the grille, blackened decorative wheel nuts and a new decal on the trailing edge of the bonnet. 'One always has to be careful when working on an icon,' said lead designer Salvador Warhol Jr. 'We were also careful when working on the 30P.

'We've put a lot of creative energy into the new rear decal, revising constantly before finally signing off on an entirely new nomenclatural visual statement.

'It uses a typeface that gently reflects the original Cistern badge from 1978, while also pointing to the future.

'The lines of the 30P's bodywork, from the new highlight strip backwards, now all seem to be sweeping, dynamically, towards this powerful new rear graphical element.'

Mr Warhol Jr said the blackened wheel nuts make use of paint technology never before seen on a Cistern 30P sedan. They draw the eye to make the car appear longer, lower and more European.

'We've always benchmarked ourselves against the big German makers,' said Warhol Jr, 'and I actually finalised the 2013 sketches in Munich to ensure the authenticity that has always been part of the Cistern experience.

'My plane's fuel stop was delayed anyway, so it was good to use the time in the transit lounge productively.'

The 30P's optional rear spoiler can now be ordered in matte black, giving a racier and more dynamic demeanour to the R-sports Super High-Performance variant, which continues with the same mechanical configuration as the standard sedan but with 17-inch alloy wheels and red seatbelts.

A range of alternative interior designs was studied before senior management decided the current package does everything so well it needed no major revisions.

That's not to say things have stood still in the Cistern's much-admired cockpit. A half-scale replica of the new rear decal graces the centre console, giving a more elegant feel to the space, and making the

Cistern an even more enjoyable experience from a driver or passenger's point of view.

Because safety has never been something Cistern has compromised on, revised child restraints ensure full compliance with new legislation.

On the mechanical side, the smooth and efficient four-speed automatic transmission has been retained, while engineers have deliberately chosen to stick with the well-proven 3-litre straight six on all models. This all-iron pushrod engine, which has been meeting the needs of demanding motorists for generations, brings renowned ruggedness and ease of servicing.

However, in keeping with the policy of continuous improvement, the software for the recently released fuel injection system has been re-calibrated to ensure no loss of power or torque – and without sacrificing economy.

'The new-for-2013 model builds on the strengths of the 30P,' says John Z. Cistern, managing director of Cistern Motor Corporation, 'and it has all been achieved with no change to the price.

'I'm confident that this revamp lifts our product to the next level.'

*Where it currently sits at 63.

60 Buckminster who?

Fuller, perhaps. I'm taking a guess, but among the multitudes with the given name of Buckminster, Mr Fuller probably has the strongest car connection.

He was a slightly barking, but always fascinating, philosopher, architect, designer and author.

Buckminster Fuller is most famous not just for having the nattiest name in cool-dom, but for his work on the geodesic dome.

This is a super-strong sphere (or semi-sphere) made up of small triangles, much favoured for science museums, planetariums, radar stations and secret island headquarters of movie super-villains with dreams of world domination.

He is described by the Buckminster Fuller Institute as a 'renowned twentieth-century inventor and visionary' who 'dedicated his life to making the world work for all of humanity.'

Fuller was certainly associated with a car that was inventive and visionary, but it stiffed at the box office. And for very good reasons.

Strange fish: the Dymaxion car.

Dymaxion draws a crowd.

Fuller called it the Dymaxion, abbreviating *dynamic*, *maximum* and *tension*. He used the same term for the Dymaxion Home and even Dymaxion Sleep, a system of short naps which he claimed allowed him to be up-and-about twenty-two hours a day.

Fuller built three prototype cars, known as Dymaxion Car #1, Dymaxion Car #2 and Berryl. OK, that third one was a ruse. It was really Dymaxion Car #3.

In July 1933 the first of them was shown at the Century of Progress Exhibition in Chicago. Like the later cars, it was a three-wheeler and shaped like an elongated teardrop. Or, less politely, a cockroach with an eating disorder.

The second car is the only one that survives and is now held up as a landmark example of yesterday's vision of tomorrow.

It influenced the real mainstream aero-cars that appeared later in the 1930s (which also failed in the marketplace). The Dymaxion, though, didn't stop with streamlining. Some reports say it had a driver's seatbelt. The rear-view mirror was a periscope, an idea that resurfaced decades later.

It had lightweight construction and front-wheel drive. All three wheels steered, making it a whiz for parking.

The lone rear wheel was designed to leave the ground at speeds above 90 mph (145 km/h) to reduce rolling resistance. Yes, really. As a modern driver might say: *It does what? How the flying fluffy duck do I get out of this thing?*

Fuller, born in 1895, apparently spent his early years stumbling from university to university and job to job, dealing with depression and poverty. He then had a vision that he should make his life 'an experiment to find what a single individual can contribute to changing the world and benefitting all humanity'. Rather than writing self-help books, he did something of actual worth. He gifted us an explosion of ideas, some of them very good. And then there was the car …

Buckminster Fuller.

Fuller wanted some sort of science-fiction propulsion device, but had to make do with a Ford V8. Still, he promised 120 mph (193 km/h) and 30 mpg (7.8 L/100 km), suggesting it wasn't only the Dymaxion's trailing wheel that wasn't firmly planted on the ground.

Such a top speed would put the Dymaxion up with the best sports cars of the day, but it was actually closer to a mini bus: nearly 6 metres long with no fewer than eleven seats.

Three months after its unveiling, Car #1 crashed, killing the driver and injuring two passengers. Many blamed the weird-arse chassis, though probably not in those words.

Would-be investors held on to their funds. Fuller spent his inheritance building a third car. It made the newsreels and the covers of many magazines, but no one would finance series production.

In the 1960s, Fuller argued the Dymaxion wasn't a car but the 'land-taxiing phase of a wingless, twin-orientable jet stilts flying device'. He died in 1983, presumably still without anyone having a clue what the hell he was talking about.

61 The worst thing on wheels

In the future, the turret-free tank known as the Hummer may become as famous as the Edsel or P76 as a symbol of where it all went wrong. Yet for General Motors, it once seemed a perfect fit.

In the late 1990s it purchased the rights to use the design and to market a range of vehicles under the Hummer brand. Interest in a street-legal version had started after the 1991 Gulf War with the sight of victorious US troops driving into Kuwait in these oddly proportioned, ultra-macho vehicles.

GM accountants couldn't stop smiling: as an unashamed military vehicle, the brand could celebrate crudity, bombast and a lack of style. The products could be built cheap, priced dear, rarely needed to be updated and required no pretence of mechanical sophistication.

Marketers could easily reach much of the potential audience by advertising in specialist magazines such as *Soldier of Fortune* and *Machine Gun Enthusiast*. GM's US divisions were already light truck specialists, which in a Detroit context meant they were *already building other vehicles using Flintstones technology*. For its Hummer models, GM engineers could reuse the weighty, inefficient, cheaply built mechanical components they were already putting into the 2.5-tonne Chevy pick-up-cum-battering rams sold to mums and dads as 'the perfect runabout'.

GM management really must have thought 'someone has to wake up to this lurk' but, no, Hummer orders kept flooding in.

And, hey, if fuel was priced at 26 cents per litre (as it then was), and you had no concern for other road users let alone the rest of the world, why wouldn't any self-respecting good ol' boy buy a Hummer?

Not every American loved it, however. A website called fuh2.com collated nearly 5000 photos of people flipping the bird in the direction of the Hummer. It also included poetry, such as 'Haiku by Tim':

Hulking black Hummer
Purchased in rank atonement
Small peckered driver

Unfortunately, the Hummer story didn't stop with the US. In 2006, just two weeks after a highly publicised survey by *The Lancet* found that 654,695 people had died in Iraq since the start of the 2003 invasion, Holden announced it was going to sell the ultimate piece of Gulf War chic Down Under.

Australians too immediately lined up for this surprisingly unroomy box on wheels. When it was criticised for its profligacy, Holden's marketing people shot back with, 'But the Hummer H3 is no bigger or thirstier than a Toyota Prado.' This is called the 'I didn't kill any more people than Ivan Milat' defence.

Holden also boasted it was the ultimate lifestyle vehicle, yet almost every single one you saw was covered with so much of the optional bling it would almost certainly never leave a sealed road. Most owners looked the wrong shape to have a lifestyle anyway.

The original road-going Hummer.

Of course the world eventually woke up to the Hummer, which, by the time of the GFC in 2007, was considered only slightly more desirable than eczema. Holden began furiously selling all its stock as 'demos' (yeah, right) at *simply crazy prices you can't afford to miss.* GM in the US tried to offload the entire brand (without success) as it struggled and eventually succumbed to bankruptcy.

When some future archaeologist digs up a Hummer he may conclude that 65 million years after the dinosaurs were wiped out by a meteor, General Motors was wiped out by a dinosaur.

62 Is that absolutely the truth?*

- Double world champion Scottish F1 driver Jimmy Clark (born James C. Clarke) was the nephew of science fiction writer Arthur C. Clarke and always carried a copy of his uncle's breakthrough 1951 novel *The Sands of Mars* in his open-wheelers as a good luck charm.

- The 1946 Fiat 300, a planned rival for the 2CV, had a space-frame chassis made entirely of dried pasta. Early road-testers reported structural rigidity issues, particularly in the wet. The project was eventually scrapped in favour of the bigger, non-food-based 600 model.

- Although it is widely known that Audi's road cars are named after standard paper trim sizes (A3, A4, A5, etc.), it is less publicised that its off-road/SUV models take their designations from medieval cuts of cloth. A Q7, for example, was a bolt of fabric measuring the same width as Henry VIII's outstretched arms.

- Mitsubishi Motors Australia Limited plans to increase revenues by re-introducing the Magna as a premium ice-cream. Versions will include vanilla, white chocolate, almond and Ralliart Sports.

- Australian explorer Nobby Crankhurst, famous for his incredible strength and endurance, and complete lack of mechanical comprehension, set out in 1916 to be the first man to drive a car across the Great Sandy Desert. When he couldn't work out how to start the engine of the four-cylinder British-made Alldays and Onion 12/14 tourer supplied by a sponsor for the expedition, he became the first man to push a car across the Great Sandy Desert.

- Subaru's original boxer engine had three cylinders on one side, and one on the other. At high revs, it tended to exit out the left side of the car.

- Among the most obscure VWs is the Royal Tennis. Placed between the Golf and Polo, this 1988 effort sold poorly and was soon discontinued. Even then, it was more successful than the smallest VW hatch of all time, the Squash.

- The second most iconic muscle car photo in Australian magazine history is the in-car shot of a Valiant Charger E49 at an indicated 143 mph on a level crossing outside a kindergarten. After publishing management intervened, the original photo was retouched so that the red traffic light appeared amber.

- The people of the British Isles were the only Europeans not to invent the wheel. Circular devices capable of revolving around an axle had to be imported from Germany and, at times, France right up until the closure of the MG Rover Group in 2005. Spies in MI5's industrial division finally acquired engineering drawings from a former East German double agent in early 2007.

*No, not even nearly.

HISTORICAL NOTES
63 On the nose

The lady was no tramp. She just lacked class. Not the type you can acquire either, the type you have to be born with. Apparently.

Still, the 'beautiful and provocative' Eleanor Thornton remains the most famous half-naked lady ever to adorn the nose of a car.

She was the model, or at least the inspiration, for the Spirit of Ecstasy (otherwise known as the flying lady or 'Ellie in her Nightie'),

which has adorned Rolls-Royce radiators for slightly more than 100 years.

Thornton had an Australian father, a Spanish mother and the middle name Velasco. Her journey from London secretary to grille ornament began in the late nineteenth century when she worked for a man named Claude Johnson at the newly formed Automobile Club.

She left there in 1902 to work at a very early motor magazine, *The Car Illustrated*, run by John Walter Edward Douglas-Scott Montagu, soon to become the second Lord Montagu of Beaulieu.

A grubby profession such as magazine publishing wasn't considered déclassé for a man such as Montagu, as long as it was about products the common people couldn't afford (automobiles) or activities they were excluded from (the hunt). *The Car Illustrated* often brought the two together.

Anyway, during one of the occasional bouts of heterosexuality and outbreeding that afflict the English upper classes, Montagu commenced an affair with Thornton.

While all this was happening, Johnson – he of the Automobile Club – had partnered up with two rather different characters: Charles Rolls, a toff with lots of money, and Henry Royce, a perfectionist engineer without much at all.

Johnson was in many ways the marketing brain behind the company they formed, and is often referred to as the hyphen in Rolls-Royce. Montagu was an early client for the brand – they all moved in the same circles – and considered the Parthenon grille on his car too bare. He commissioned an artist working at *The Car Illustrated*, Charles Robinson Sykes, to do something about it.

The 1923 Silver Ghost.

The result was a mascot called 'The Whisperer'. It was much like the famous Spirit, except for two details. Firstly, Ellie seemed to have sadly misplaced her nightie. Secondly, she had a finger across her lips, as if to hush up the unseemly affair (Montagu was married at the time, and of course not to some magazine secretary; his wife was the daughter of the 7th Marquess of Lothian).

Johnson thought that, with a bit of cleaning up, Montagu's mascot would make a fine emblem for all Rolls-Royce cars. Sykes responded with what he called 'The Spirit of Speed,' which was much closer to today's symbol.

Johnson described it, rather fruitily, as: 'A graceful little goddess … who has selected road travel as her supreme delight and alighted on the prow of a Rolls-Royce motor car to revel in the freshness of the air and the musical sound of her fluttering draperies.'

However, he thought it should be called 'The Spirit of Ecstasy'. Well, Johnson did hang around in clubs (even if they were automobile clubs).

The Spirit of Ecstasy was available as an official option for Rolls-Royce cars from 1911 and soon became standard equipment.

Although the inspiration for the be-winged symbol was not in doubt, and Thornton often did model for Sykes, some believe that the body in question wasn't Thornton's. Though no gentleman would say how he knew.

The story didn't end well for her. She had to give up for adoption her daughter by Montagu, and in 1915, Thornton drowned along with about 342 other passengers when the SS *Persia* was torpedoed by a U-Boat. She was thirty-five.

Rolls-Royce itself could have died on several occasions afterwards but was regularly thrown a life-buoy. This was not because it made money (often it didn't) but because it was such a powerful brand. Quite a bit of that was down to the flapping lady on the radiator.

Today's Parthenon Grille, with Nelly still atop.

64 What do old engineers say?

It is very exciting to be here on this thirtieth anniversary. Thank you very much for talking to me. Now, you were the head of engineering in 1983 when Maserrari won the championship with the revolutionary ninety-six valve …

It started long before that. I was looking for a job. We had just come out of a war, of course, and we were very poor and there was no work and my father said to me, 'Down the street lives The Great Lambardi. You should talk to him.' You know who that is?

Well …

Yes, Carlo Lambardi, the genius who designed the rear suspension on the legendary 42P Grand Prix Special of 1933 with the transverse …

Ah yes, that Lambardi. Fascinating. Now I just want to wind forward to the 1980s, because it really is a terrific story …

And Lambardi said to me, he said, 'Why did you come here?' I was just a boy, but the words came out: 'I want to be as great an engineer as you.' I didn't even know what engineers did, and I never even dreamed that one day … but Lambardi liked my face. He said, 'I'll talk to *il Commandatore*.'

And so, to cut a long story short, you became Maserrari GP engineering director in 1968 and then just fourteen years later …

Well, I'll tell you, *Il Commandatore*, he looked from across his big desk and said, 'What does it take to be a great engineer … a great engineer for Scuderia Maserrari?' I stuttered a little – no one in our village owned a motor vehicle – and he said, 'Massimo, you are quiet, but I like your face. Tomorrow you start in the workshop. You sweep the floor.'

So anyway, the 1980s. The 96V. That's what this anniversary is about …

I was ready to leave at the end of the first day – this must be, June, yes, June in 1950.

Very interesting … but I've been promised just ten minutes, so if we can …

No, August. I remember clearly because the Italian Grand Prix was two weeks away and Alessandro Bortalotti threw at me twelve pistons, one by one, yelling the whole time. It was nothing to do with my sweeping, which I did *perfetto*. It was the team's preparations. Bortalotti was the engine designer – you know that, don't you? – the very first one at the company. And this is something that has never been published before. Listen closely: Bortalotti stole that engine design from Nino Marcolli who also worked there then. You know Marcolli?

I've seen the name, but I must ask …

Marcolli told me – even though I was new – that he would never again work with Bortalotti. Or Maserrari. Not for one minute more. Marcolli was a very passionate man. He was upset because Bortalotti took the credit for his engine. And because Ferrati Maserrari, *il Commandatore*, was sleeping with his wife and six daughters. I was only a boy and I didn't know what to say. Marcolli looked me in the eye and said, 'I am leaving the company and I want to take you with me.' He liked the way I swept.

So, if we just move a little beyond those early days, I'm very interested in the long and, I believe, very fraught development of that technically fascinating, championship winning, 1983 car …

I thought about Marcolli's offer. My father, he said, 'What would the Great Lambardi think?' Luckily I stayed because, as we all know, Marcolli designed the 341G monoposto then he was killed while testing it. That was 1951. By then Bortalotti was dead too and I was allowed to clean the carburettors.

The PR handler is giving me the sign to wind up. So it looks like we didn't quite …

Well, you are very rude. You keep interrupting. You have a lot to learn about interviewing.

65 A quick look at the Welsh

In terms of car-making, the Welsh have done more than you may think. Though not necessarily a *great deal* more. And perhaps less than some other European countries, such as Germany and Italy.

Still, as someone descended from very short coal miners who could sing, it gives me pleasure to explain the rich history of the homegrown Welsh automobile.

It must be said, though, that it's rich in detail rather than, say, rich in extent, or success or acclaim.

The number of companies that have designed and produced series production road cars in that country totals, broadly speaking, one.

Yes, one. It is ironic that there have been more cars created in New South Wales than in Old All Wales.

So what is that one Welsh car? It's the Gilbern, first seen in 1959.

Company founder Giles Smith was a butcher who, like most butchers (one imagines), dreamt of making his own luxurious GT coupe as he boned lamb and eviscerated pork.

Progress was made when he met Bernard Friese, a former prisoner of war (if his name didn't give it away, Herr Friese was playing for the away team). The German had expertise in fibreglass and the pair planned out a one-off vehicle with Austin A35 mechanicals and a badge combining bits of their names, 'Gil and Bern'. They built it in

Above and below: Gilbern GT 1800.

the back of the butcher shop. A tree had to be removed so it could be driven out.

When it was suggested by others that it looked just like a bought one, Gilbern set up shop in Llantwit Fardre, Pontypridd, to see if anyone really would buy one.

The operation started with about five people spitting out one car kit per month. That first model was the GT, with a 2+2 cabin and an optional Coventry Climax 1.1-litre engine. Complete cars were soon sold, eventually with MG 1.5-, 1.6- and 1.8-litre engines.

The Gilbern GT was a good-looking car for its time, was well reviewed and the price came in at under a thousand quid, which sounds like good value. Apparently it wasn't. It was considered dear and only 280 were built in eight years.

The replacement, known as the Genie, was bigger and more expensive, which didn't exactly help the cause. Again though, it had vaguely Italian styling and reasonable fit and finish. There were still plenty of MG components, though the engine was now the Ford Capri V6.

The Invader, a reworked Genie, came out in 1969 and, with just over 600 examples made, was the best selling of all. However, when you're losing money on every car sold, an increase in sales isn't always a good thing.

The harder edged T11 coupe, painted yellow and looking like a wedge of gouda, was unveiled in 1971 to try to provide a new direction. Alas, the old direction – down – prevailed.

The T11 remained a one-off. The Gilbern company changed hands a couple of times before belly flopping in 1973.

In 2009 Cardiff band The Keys recorded the song 'A Brief History of Gilbern Cars Ltd', taking its inspiration from, er, you can probably guess. It sounds like a Black Sabbath outtake, which is not how every manufacturer would want to be remembered.

The use of MG and Ford of Britain components doesn't suggest long life, though Gilbern enthusiasts say of the 1005 examples built, about 500 are still on the road. No doubt they'll be removed when the tow trucks arrive.

What about the Scots and Irish then? Scotland produced the Argyll, the Hillman Imp and perhaps the worst electric car ever made, the Scamp.

Ireland was responsible for the fibreglass bodied Shamrock (projected volume: 10,000 per year; actual volume: eight, ever) and, twenty years later, the ill-conceived, ill-built, ill-fated DeLorean.

Meanwhile, there's regular talk of new Welsh road cars: the leaning NARO from the Narrow Car Company, for instance. And the Connaught Type-D, which looks like a fairly typical sedan-based two-door, except there's no sedan to go with it. The biggest surprise is that it's powered by an 'inhouse built' V10 engine. Well, I'll be llanfairpwllgwyngylled!

The Connaught name comes from the famous British racing brand (via tenuous connections) and we're told a hybrid version will follow. Which is ambitious, since the non-hybrid Type-D still doesn't seem to be on sale.

HISTORICAL NOTES
66 The lowdown on Studebaker

Studebaker is a word that was used in Middle English to denote an ornamental nose guard or, sometimes, a codpiece.

Actually, that's not true. Nor is a Studebaker a type of kiln, a plug of tobacco shaped to fit in a traditional Swedish pipe made from elk bone, or an inflammation of the oesophagus.

It's the surname of a bunch of big-bearded brothers of German descent, who lived in America in the 1800s. Their company started out making horse-drawn wagons. The first Studebaker car was produced circa 1902, with electric power.

Why are we discussing it, more than 110 years since the first car was built, and nearly half a century since the last (in Canada not the US, curiously)? Because the brand is back. Sort of.

The Studebaker of old rarely took the path most trodden. It named one of its models Dictator during the 1930s. It called a sparsely equipped,

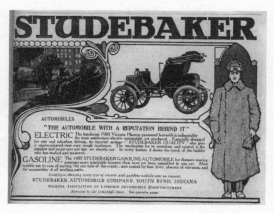

low-cost special The Scotsman. It built a truck called Weasel, and a Land Cruiser before Toyota.

The corporation had an excruciatingly long death that wouldn't have been out of place in opera. But somewhere in between all that, it was at the forefront of American car-making, ushering in a golden age of design from very soon after World War II.

Studebaker achieved its early design-led successes under the guidance of the legendary stylist Raymond Loewy. There was also the flamboyant Vigil Exner, and the underrated Robert Bourke. Maybe Bourke's problem was, in that company, his name was just too ordinary.

The Starlight coupe of 1947 was described by many as the car Buck Rogers would drive. (If you don't remember Studebaker, Mr Rogers is

Studebaker Champion.

Studebaker Hawk.

probably even more obscure.) The clean lines and massive wrap-around rear glasshouse of the Starlight gave it a 'coming or going?' look, and the Bullet Nose (from 1950) seem to point straight at the future.

Superbly styled, European-influenced (though American-sized) models appeared in 1953. Even into the 1960s – by which stage financial troubles were immense – Studebaker design stood out.

The Lark coupe of 1962 looked more like a Mercedes of the era than a Chevrolet. Most striking of all was the Avanti, a two-door fibreglass coupe that brought Raymond Loewy back into the 'Studie' fold after a few years away.

The Avanti looked like nothing else, though not everyone thought in a good way. It's still held up by many as a classic that deserved much more; fewer than 5000 originals were made, though replicas have been turned out by others ever since.

The Studebaker Motor Company was relaunched in Colorado, circa 2010, under the slogan: 'Out to build the best vehicle on the road.' Confidence was undermined just a little with the website disclaimer: 'Studebaker Motor Company is not yet able to produce vehicles, as we are in the planning stages. However, we are almost ready to sell Studebaker shirts and hats.'

How the Studebaker name was acquired is unclear but the chief executive, one R.W. Reed, announced plans to reintroduce the Lark, Hawk, President and Champ in modern form.

First, he said, the company would sell 50 cc scooters. This progression, Reed pointed out, was similar to Honda's.

The elaborate mock-ups on the Studebaker site (www.studebaker motorcompany.com) included a modern hatch that did not do a lot to earn the name 'Studebaker Lark', a so-so SUV and a 'sports sedan' that looked like the automotive design equivalent of a typo.

Confidence was undermined just that little bit further when one clicked through to the link of the official distributor of Studebaker scooters, the Kahuna Trading Company. It was a gruesomely

Studebaker Lark.

amateurish website mainly flogging cheap dresses and Hawaiian shirts. Mr Reed doubled as a tee-shirt model.

The mock-ups were later removed from the site and it was announced that there would be no motorcycles. The cars would come first. On the evidence so far, nothing much is going to happen quickly.

BASED ON A TRUE STORY

67 What does the new MD say?

Ladies and gentlemen of the press, it's a pleasure to be here in Austria, and I'd like to thank you for agreeing to have this media conference in my mother tongue.

I am sure in the fullness of time I will come to understand your language but, until then, it is refreshing that so many of you are happy to speak English.

It is no exaggeration to say there are terrific opportunities for our cars in Austria – sorry, Australia – I do get the two mixed up but I know only one has kangaroos. And I'll have my new PA check which one that is.

Either way, this country and our brand go back a long way.

During the flight I took the trouble to listen to the abridged talking-book version of our corporate history and it records much about this long-running and important relationship.

It was our 'Downunder' division that set up the first successful transfer pricing system back in the 1960s.

It was here in the 1970s that we shipped the tooling for those engines that no longer met stringent overseas pollution regulations. This otherwise would have had to be scrapped, or expensively modified.

It was here that the government paid us generously to assemble cars, and then paid us more when we said we were going to leave, then more again when we agreed to import fully assembled cars, pull them down to the last nut and bolt and rebuild them.

Our slogan 'Reassembled for Australian Conditions' has become a mainstay of our marketing campaign in this country and I feel it is the bedrock of our great success and unique rapport with the people of Austria. Sorry. *Australia*.

And it is to this country that head office has built up a long tradition of sending ambitious but not-quite-good-enough executives as some sort of compensation for not getting the job they thought they deserved, but were never really going to be considered for.

That of course has ended. They assure me.

Enough about the past. People are asking what I will be doing with this operation. Well, I have three words: growth, growth and growth. And cost-cutting.

OK, that's four words, maybe even five. But I'm confident the efficiencies will have no negative effect at the retail interface.

That's because we can leverage our synergies, and action exciting customer-focussed initiatives based on learnings, and create long-term strategies to, er, effect solutions. To things.

I want to expand our model line-up too, perhaps even introduce vehicles with fuel-injection and disc brakes.

Our company, I think, has never really done enough to stress its technology credentials and I want to change that. For example, we are undisputed leaders in those little black dots that they put along the edges of glassware these days.

And significantly, we have exclusive access to a unique three-wheel drive system out of China, which is very cost-effective – my god *is it cheap*! – yet which offers 50 per cent more traction than the conventional two-wheel drive systems we are currently offering.

I'm excited about it and I think you'll see it as a practical way to cope with Australia's unique circumstances: the high mountains, the snowy winters, the monsoons …

The same company reckons it can get a bolt-on hybrid system up and running for us in the next few months too. So we'll certainly be speaking to that in our 'environmental leadership' media campaign that starts tomorrow.

But most of all, and perhaps we could just go off the record briefly here, my main focus as the new managing director of this subsidiary will be the usual one: to produce impressive short-term results and get the hell back to head office.

Still, it could have been New Zealand.

68 Matters Antipodean

1. During what decade was the last Australian Valiant made: the 1960s, the 1970s or the 1980s?

2. In the 1959 doomsday flick *On the Beach*, a nuclear scientist achieved his life's ambition by winning what was described in the film as 'the 1964 Australian Grand Prix at Phillip Island'. What unlikely actor played the boffin-cum-GP star?

3. A locally built 'Australianised' version of the Mini Minor, released in 1969, was known as the Morris Mini K. What did the K stand for?

4. The English REDeX company was trying to promote what type of product when it sponsored the famous 'Around Australia Trials' of the mid-1950s? And in what three years were the original REDeX Trials run?

5. Ford Australia's LTD brand name was an acronym of what? Clue: it has nothing to do with 'Limited'.

6. What was the name of the founder of the McLaren Formula One team, in what country was he born, and what F1 record did he set in December 1959?

7. A 1977 Australian film starring Paul Couzens, Eva Dickinson and Sigrid Thornton, and set in western Sydney, was not only named after a car, it had a theme song sung by a man with a remarkably similar name to the car *and* the film. What was it?

8. Two winners of the Australian Grand Prix have given their names to special 'sporting' versions of mass-produced Australian cars – one in the 1960s and one in the 1970s. Who were they and what were the cars?

9. What Japanese vehicle shares its name with a town in southern New South Wales? And for an extra point – not that we're really giving out any points, but dream on – what mountain had an Australian-built Austin named after it?

10. For motor-sport tragics: Five Australian racing drivers have competed in International Formula One GP races in Brabham cars. Name them.

NB: Answers are on page 318.

69 All the fun of the world's fastest roller coaster

Ferrari World in Abu Dhabi is advertised as the world's biggest indoor theme park.

It's also the site of the Formula Rossa roller coaster. This will accelerate from zero to 100 in two seconds flat and keep accelerating to an all-time coaster record of 240 km/h.

By then just 4.9 seconds have elapsed. The 2.1-kilmometre track is inspired, it is said, by the Monza F1 circuit.

If that's not enough, the nearby G-Force ride straps you into a Ferrari seat and blasts you 62 metres into the air with 3.8 times the force of gravity.

So what's it all like, I hear you ask. And I'd be a good bloke to tell since I succeeded in sprinting off to Ferrari World during a brief stop-over in Abu Dhabi.

Now, anyone could just turn up and describe the experience, humorously itemising exactly what they threw up before, during and afterwards. But I wanted to take this seriously, to enter the arena of fire fully versed in the history, the ethos, the very fabric of roller-coaster culture. A scholar of the art form, no less.

I followed roller-coaster history right back to Russia in the 1400s. Gravity-powered capsules were apparently first used for fun and leisure on specially built ice tracks outside St Petersburg, though with sleds below rather than wheels.

In 1884, at New York's Coney Island, a device known as the Switch-Back Railway opened for business. Although straight and pretty slow, the 180-metre-long undulating carriage ride probably counts as the first modern-style roller coaster.

The designer, the extravagantly named LaMarcus Adna Thompson, built about fifty more across the US. Other non-Thompson roller coasters appeared too, Stateside and in Europe.

Opposite: Ferrari World reaches out across Abu Dhabi.
Above: The world's fastest (and possibly most photoshopped) roller coaster.

From 1912 the 'upstop' wheel was introduced, clamping the coaster cars to the tracks and allowing extreme rides to become far more so (though not more dangerous, as the locking safety bar for passengers soon followed).

Roller coasters competed against each other for the severity of their ups, downs, twists and turns, and the silliness of their names (The Thriller, The Wildcat and, wait for it, California Screamin').

The technology to bank turns at 90 degrees arrived in the early 1970s. The Corkscrew at Knott's Berry Farm in California introduced the barrel roll in 1975. Its stomach-emptying qualities were replicated at Sea World, Queensland, in the early 1980s.

The Revolution (at California's Magic Mountain) gave roller-coastees the first full loop-the-loop in 1976.

Pre-Formula Rossa, the highest speed coaster was the Kingda Ka in New Jersey with a claimed 206 km/h. Laurels for the fastest accelerating go to the Dodonpa at Fuji-Q Highland in Japan: a claimed 0–172 km/h in a dazzling 1.8 seconds.

But enough of the background; it was time to sample the coaster with the most-er, at least in terms of outright speed.

The taxi skirted the Yas Marina Formula One circuit, took a right and we were there at Ferrari World with its enormous atrium, its 86,000 square metre floor space, its rows of speakers playing the sounds of high-performance engines, its authentic Ferrari road and race cars and its prominent sign:

'Due to our maintenance requirements, the following rides are unavailable: Formula Rossa, G-Force.'

70 The weirdest French cars

We could list the best French cars, and there are plenty of impressive candidates, but that wouldn't be playing to their national strengths, now would it? What the French do, perhaps better than anyone, is weird. *Comme ça*:

Citroën DS – Obvious, yes. But beautiful and revolutionary and much else as well. Right down to the brakes, steering and suspension. Weird, as in wonderful.

Citroën 2CV – Equally obvious. And equally elegant in terms of answering a query, in this case: how do you build an ultra-cheap car that can carry four people and a basket of eggs across a freshly ploughed field without any breakages. Well, someone had to ask the hard questions.

Citroen Ami 6 Break and Citroen DS.

Citroën Ami 6 – The last double-chevron car we have room for. Alas, this boxy sedan, with deep-sea marine creature styling details, was weird solely as in *weird*.

Panhard Dyna Z – Who thought Panhard would work as a name? The first n is silent, the h isn't pronounced and the final letter is dropped, leaving very little worth saying. The 1954 Dyna Z with its inset eyes, pursed lips grille and rounded flanks was strange. Even stranger: the 1948 Panhard-Levassor Coach Dynavia, a streamliner with a central headlight that seemed to be set within a gramophone speaker.

Renault Megane – The 2002 model had a curved and upright rear windscreen, something that hadn't been seen in generations. Nobody else would have dared. Wonderful!

Renault Avantime – If the Megane was wonderfully adventurous, this was daftly so. A coupe built around a people-mover body shell, it was described as being ahead of its time (that's what the name alluded to). We're still not ready for it. In the same year (2001) Renault shocked everyone with the Vel Satis luxury car. These days it doesn't look quite as scary as it did. Which is not to excuse it. It's still out there.

Renault Twizzy – Has anything as refreshingly oddball ever come from a mainstream manufacturer as this reimagining of the electric car and the bubble car?

Inter Berline – Just one look is all it takes. This 1950s bubble car was meant to be a Messerschmitt competitor. Despite the looks, it didn't float, though the front wheel

Inter 175A Berline.

and axle assemblies folded for easy storage.

Helicron – Several propeller-driven cars came from France, including the 1932 Helicron, possibly because the French considered themselves the pioneers of aviation. There was usually no shield over the prop; better pedestrians be julienned than aerodynamic efficiency foregone.

Voisin Biscuter – Gabriel Voisin built aeroplanes as well as bizarre and occasionally stunningly beautiful luxury cars. He also designed the ugly automotive runt known as Biscuter. It made the 2CV look like a limo and was eventually built in Spain, perhaps being too weird even for the French.

Voisin Biscuter prototype and Voisin Biscuter C31.

Matra 530 – The styling of this polyester-bodied 1960s sportster was *avant-garde. Trop* so. The bodywork started low and seemed to fall away at every point. It had a targa roof too, before Porsche gave the removable panels their name.

Claveau – Some radical and fascinating cars wore this badge, including a mid-engined 1927 streamliner that looked only 5 per cent less like a cockroach than a cockroach did.

Bugatti Type 32 – Bugatti built some of the most graceful moving objects of all time – and this pre-war, roller-top desk-nosed race-car. It was known as 'the Tank', probably generously. Success – and love – eluded it, but it will not be forgotten.

Pussycar l'Automodule – OK, not a production car – just a wild flight of fancy by Jean Pierre Ponthieu, a French engineer apparently known as 'the Dali of the automobile'. He called it the 'car of the year 2000'; others saw it as oh so 1960s (and *oh so* French). It could swivel into tight spots and rear like a horse. Even with that ability, its 250 cc engine might not have been enough to storm the Bastille.

Pussycar Automodule.

71 Are women smarter car buyers than men?

There could be an argument made that, if you look at the ludicrous amounts of money that some women spend on barely usable shoes and cosmetics ascribed with magical properties, they are highly unlikely to suddenly demonstrate qualities of good sense and value when buying a car. However, I'm not game for a minute to make such an argument.

I'm merely throwing it up for discussion, and then running away as fast as possible, lest someone should accuse me of misogyny, or of doubting that Clinique's Anti-Gravity Firming Eye Lift Cream really can defy Newton's laws.

Anyway, it's not all in one direction. Any thorough researcher could probably find an inciden or two in the past couple of millennia where men have also spent money on things that, on balance, could not be considered entirely sensible.

So here's a theory. Being a smart buyer is not about gender, it's about disinterest. Whether male or female, the only purchasers who are completely rational are those with absolutely no emotional investment in their purchase.

Ever bought a dishwasher? I bet you never found yourself asking 'What will owning this model say about me?', or 'Is it better than next-door's?' And I hope you didn't admire the sweep of the door's leading edge and start thinking, 'I could enjoy just sitting and looking at this. Sexy cutlery tray, too.'

Dishwashers don't do that to you, no matter how bright their brightwork, or innovatively styled those spinning things that distribute the water, mid-cycle. All that matters with a dishwasher are things such as price, dimensions, features list, energy consumption and length of warranty.

With any vehicle, however, there are so many more important things, as any buyer knows. But there's no reason that a male (to take a gender at random) can't be just as unemotional when buying a car as when buying a dishwasher.

Consider the case of a family man with an FPV Falcon brochure in hand. Listen to what he talks about when he gets home: the large boot, the generous rear seat, the towing capacity. How, when driven very,

very gently, the V8's fuel economy is surprisingly close to that of the six-cylinder mum-and-dad model (during a police pursuit, admittedly).

The typical man – in this writer's experience at least – would never be seduced just because the car that just happens to be perfect for his growing family also develops enough kilowatts to power a small city. And he'd never let his personal insecurities lean him towards a vehicle with styling that, in subtlety terms, could only be compared with the florist called 'Give Her One Tonight'.

Well come on, it's not like the potential buyer hasn't sought a second opinion. The salesman, with twenty years' experience in the industry, was able to reinforce his contention that this purchase makes perfect financial sense … that it would actually be a disastrous decision not to go ahead, what with this special deal available only this weekend, and only on this one example.

'You've worked hard. You deserve it! It's an investment … an investment in yourself.'

And to think he'd considered the less powerful model, and risked a life tinged with regret!

So emotionally uninvolved is this man likely to be, he will decide to pay extra hard-earned dollars for the larger wheel-and-tyre package to reduce his slip angles and thereby improve family safety. He'll even buy the Conrod Straight-proven mega rear-airdam to ensure utmost stability under cornering when dropping the children to school.

Could you expect a woman to be that sensible and considered? Well, as I said, I'm just throwing a few ideas around.

72 Jack Brabham's star turn

Our very own triple world champion was a movie star. Really. We all know he was a bit player in *Grand Prix*, the 1966 John Frankenheimer film, along with Bruce McLaren, Jim Clark and other F1 luminaries of the day.

But Jack merely played himself, which meant he looked very serious, didn't talk much and didn't move his mouth when he did.

By contrast, he was a properly credited actor in an earlier film known as *The Green Helmet*.

So what is *The Green Helmet*? It's a pretty standard-issue racing movie with the shoutline: 'The men who love speed, and the girls who love them.' There's some good spliced-in footage of Le Mans, Sebring and Mille Miglia sports car races – and there's Jack.

The plot (Australia's Jon Cleary turned out the screenplay based on his 1957 novel) centres around English driver Greg Rafferty, who is on the skids, all too often literally. The part is played by Bill Travers, who doesn't seem to be acting so much as getting in the way of the camera. Still, he drives the streets in a very elegant Gordon Keeble coupe, which was still a couple of years from launch (this was a hand-built prototype).

How did Jack go in the big dramatic scenes? Well, early on he merely played himself, which meant he looked very serious, didn't talk much and didn't move his mouth when he did.

But he said far more than in *Grand Prix*, even if it was necessary to rewind to make out his first lines.

'Did he run out of road?' he asks Greg Rafferty after an apparently fatal Le Mans accident. 'You going on? See you on the dawn patrol.'

Rafferty's faithful old mechanic is Sid James, playing an Australian incapable of completing a sentence without the word 'sport' in it. (For the record, the cockney star of those interminable *Carry On* films was really a South African.)

When Rafferty is offered the chance to revive his career by driving on a new American tyre that is '30 per cent less likely to skid,' he grabs it. He's teamed at Sebring with Brabham, who warns him about those tyres: 'Watch 'em on the fast corners, they break away very easy.'

OK, it's not *Hamlet*, but it's not *Days of Thunder* or *Redline* either and, by this stage of the proceedings, the very youthful Jack is quite enjoying himself. This might be because he and Rafferty were in a birdcage Maserati while their main rival – Carlo, a cardboard cut-out Latin supplied by the Department of Racial Stereotype Reinforcement – drove a standard Corvette.

Spoiler alert: Brabham and Rafferty win, but the endgame for the English driver and the American tyres is victory at the Mille Miglia. This is a big ask, since the last one had run in 1957 (as a full-on road race, at least) and this is clearly circa 1960–61. Well, it made sense in the book.

Jack Brabham (left) and Bill Travers in *The Green Helmet*.

It was in the Mille Miglia (of course) that Rafferty's father was killed. Not only are Rafferty's nerves shot, but circumstances mean his little brother – who has faithfully promised his mother he won't race – must be in the car too as navigator.

If you made this stuff up, no one would believe it. Oh, hang on …

73 Any corrections to issue?

- In a road test last Saturday, this publication stated the Aston-Martin V12 engine had a capacity of 5.93 litres. The correct figure is 5.94 litres.
- A news article published last week misnamed the paint colour on the Peugeot 508 sedan. The official designation is Thorium Grey, not Thyroid Grey.
- A Land Rover story two weeks ago used the term 'Victoria Beckham'. We apologise for any offence caused.
- A print story from last month about the continuing success of the Ford Falcon said that black is white. It isn't.
- Our extensive interview with Jackie Stewart included a very short sentence in which he talked about something other than himself. This sentence was accidentally transposed from another article and this paper accepts that the words were not Stewart's.
- Our obituary of Tesla Motors chief financial officer, Peter 'The Blade' Smith, named his former high-wire trapeze partner (and later prison cell-mate) as Kevin 'The Iron Cuff' McDowell. The correct name is Kevin 'The Iron Cuff' McDougall.
- A feature story last month misreported the number of interesting things ever said by Finnish F1 driver Kimi Räikkönen. The correct number is one.

- The caption for a photo of a Hyundai executive dinner confused the name of the international director of automotive marketing with a menu item. Can you believe it? I keep telling journalists that captions are the first thing people read. Sometimes they are the only thing. You have no idea what it's like being corrections editor … trying to rescue these so-called writers. It's not as if they thank you. And readers think it means we make more mistakes than other sources, but it simply means we – as in I – are polite enough to correct them.
- A mention in a news item of the book *Selling Cars: The Ethical Approach* was made in error. We now accept no such book has ever been published. A writer's stuff-up, of course. Yet they're the heroes here. Bunch of pampered, overly duchessed menials if you ask me. Not that you did. Sorry, I'll get back to it.
- The correct name of the material used in Great Wall gear-knobs is Plutonium 239. The journalist should have read the small yellow warning sticker more closely.
- The price of $19,990 given yesterday for the SsangYong Ddildo erroneously implied it included on-road costs. This story has also been changed online. And now has two mistakes in it.
- Our description of a certain V8 Supercar racing driver as 'a talentless, be-slubbering, syphilitic idiot' should have read 'a very capable and intelligent sportsman who reads lots of books, some that don't even have pictures'. The error was caused during the production process. Which is to say it wasn't the man whose name was on top of the story, who just happened to be me filing a few quick news stories at the editor's request, because we all end up multitasking in here … and I have a new baby and a big

mortgage, and it's not like it's much fun doing what I do, and so just occasionally I can't help shooting my mouth off, but I'm a really nice guy if you meet me, so please, please don't sue.

- The recent mention of 'an overworked corrections editor who is about to effenwell strangle someone' should have read 'an overworked ex-corrections editor'. He's had enough. He's out of here. You can spell organise with a z for all he cares, invent the engine output, guess the price, mix your metaphors … in fact take your metaphors and ram them up …

Addendum: Yesterday we published a slightly deranged piece by our former corrections editor. His allegations included a suggestion that journalists are sloopy and unprofession. We humbly apologise for all concerned to any offence such suggestions might have cased.

74 The strange tale of the Dale

The 1970s provided a golden era for the miracle machine, partly because there was widespread panic about fuel shortages and road safety.

Take the Dale, for example: a three-wheeled, two-seater wedge offered by the Twentieth Century Motor Car Corporation in 1974.

It was advertised, laughably, as 'the first space age automobile'. It was also 'dollar for dollar the best car ever built,' equally as ludicrous as none had been built beyond one or possibly two very, very dodgy prototypes.

The promise was an all-up price of just $2000 and 70 mpg (3.4 L/100 km) thanks to a 'BMW' 850 cc motorcycle engine and lightweight bodywork made from some sort of new metal.

The designer was one Dale Clift (hence the car's name) but the frontman for the organisation was Geraldine Elizabeth Carmichael.

As a frontman, she had plenty of front (she claimed the Dale could be driven into a wall at 30 mph without damage to vehicle or occupants), and she also had plenty of man.

Although claiming to be a widowed mother of five, she was born (and otherwise known as) Jerry Dean Michael. Nothing wrong with that, of course, as long as it brought happiness. Problem was, wearing a dress had at least one other purpose: keeping at bay law-enforcement authorities who wanted a chat about fraud offences going back more than a decade.

While Carmichael told *Newsweek* in 'a low husky voice' that she was a genius, that she was ready to take on GM, would sell 250,000 Dales a year then expand the range, etc., she was pocketing money from investors and withholding the $3 million in fees she had apparently promised the designer.

Photographer Mike Salisbury was sent by *Car and Driver* magazine to grab some photos. He said the factory had no door, dirt floors and 'smelled of scam' while the car looked like 'a broken-off plastic airplane cockpit from a scary amusement ride'. A replica of Elvis Presley's Lincoln soon turned up and Jerry-cum-Elizabeth stepped out 'cigarette in hand ... all dressed in a pale yellow pantsuit with a voice like Broderick Crawford'. [Crawford was a raspy American tough-guy actor.]

Salisbury flicked open the bonnet for a photo and found not a BMW unit but a Briggs and Stratton lawnmower engine. 'There was no steering wheel,' he later reflected, 'no gas pedal, no glass windows.'

According to one report, the firm's PR man, an ex-con, was shot to death by another employee in the company's offices. Carmichael suddenly moved the project from California to Dallas, then disappeared.

The Dallas DA's office determined – surprise, surprise – there were never any intentions to produce the Dale car.

Carmichael, meanwhile, didn't resurface until 1989 when she unwittingly starred in the TV show 'Unsolved Mysteries' selling flowers under the name Kathryn Elizabeth Johnson. After which she/he spent time in prison.

Oh, thems were the days.

The Dale. Panel fit was one issue.

RATTLETRAPS, ETC.
75 Time for a short story

In the 1950s, 1960s and 1970s micro cars were cheap because they were flimsy and inherently unsafe. You knew that when you bought them; it was the non-cash price you paid for saving money.

These days micros tend to be disproportionately expensive because they have to meet strict safety standards – and that's not easy when there's so little to work with. Here are a few tiddlers from the days when there were no such considerations:

Mr Fitzjohn's Messerschmitt.

Messerschmitt cabin scooter – The Messerschmitt is one of the more successful micro cars – and is now considered highly collectable. This photo shows an English version, snapped during the big London bus strike of 1958 (which one, you ask). The caption reads: 'Mr Donald L. Fitzjohn of Highbury New Park … pulls into the kerb in his bubble car to offer a lift to Mrs Clark of Peckham whilst passing over the London Bridge this morning.'

Mrs Clark's answer has not been preserved. If she cared for her dignity (it would require straddling the front seat with her skirted legs) or for her safety (it would require travelling in a Messerschmitt – and with a potential letch), she would have said 'not bloody likely'.

Italjet Peppery – The early 1970s fuel crisis brought a rash of small cars, which, like most rashes, needed to be dealt with before it spread. It was unsightly and irritating and, er, I think the analogy has already been stretched much too far. But look at this and weep. It was from Italjet (better known as a scooter maker) and known as the Peppery '50 cc urban commuter'. Urban commuter? You must be …

Thanks to a rear-mounted conglomeration of steel parts

Italjet Peppery.

optimistically described as an engine, top speed was said to be 55 km/h. Such a velocity was presumably achieved in the Italian alps during a long downhill section.

BMW Isetta – There's been talk of BMW reviving the Isetta name. Which, to some, would be like the White Star Line bringing back the name Titanic. This is another news photo, showing David Mappin, a

Mr Mappin's Isetta.

self-described 'gemologist', using a state-of-the-art radio-telephone to turn his car into a mobile office in 1960. The text says that when Mappin discovered he was suddenly needed in Malta, he arranged everything – his ticket, currency et al. – on the go.

Pity Mr Mappin didn't divert some of the money he invested in high-tech communications towards a car that wasn't crap. This Isetta is a loathsome British version, which had one wheel fewer to avoid 'motor car' tax (as a three-wheeler with no reverse gear, it was considered a motorcycle). The original design used the engine (located on the right) as a counterweight to the driver, who sat on the left. As well as having one wheel fewer, the British version put engine and driver on the same side, requiring a hefty counterweight to try to balance things up. It still tipped over.

Casalini Sulky – Another early 1970s mini monstrosity, this one called Sulky. Like the Peel, it was a one-cylinder 50 cc vehicle designed to carry a single adult and his or her shopping. However, the Sulky was slightly wider than the Peel and the advertising materials hinted there was room for a second or even third occupant squeezed onto the bench seat around that centrally mounted steering wheel. Nope, can't think of any adverse safety implications there.

Must-have features included an all-steel body, a side-opening rear door with easy low loading lip and, er, ah, OK you've got us there.

There was a doorless version shown in the brochure, for those who thought the model shown here was just too luxurious.

senza targa
si guida senza patente

Sulky? You would be if you'd bought it.

Unlike most motor show specials, which were not available in stores, Italy's Casalini company sold about a thousand Sulkys per annum for several years, and the vehicle gained a fourth wheel somewhere along the way.

Casalini still produces micro cars and light commercials, including some of the world's most stunted utes.

Minissima – The year is 1973 and, by law, all motor show exhibits must have a leggy blonde draped over them (and not always a clothed one). What's more, some very daft vehicles are being exposed to daylight. This was better than many, though having the only opening window or door at the rear might have been a limitation.

The aluminium-bodied Minissima was designed by Bill Towns around Mini components. It so impressed British Leyland executives they bought the rights and did what they did with most promising concepts. They buried it.

There were four seats (the rear two inward-facing) plus a luggage area, all squeezed into an overall length of 2.29 metres. The rear door was there partly so the Minissima could be squeezed into tight spaces tail-to-curb, allowing the occupants to step straight out onto the footpath. Bad luck, though, if you needed to get out after a rear-end accident. There wasn't even a sunroof to provide an escape hatch.

Towns would go on to shape the Aston Martin Lagonda (though 'shape' might be an exaggeration) and the Jensen-Healey (oh, good grief!).

Despite owning Minissima rights, Leyland eschewed replacing the fourteen-year-old Mini with it or anything else, instead keeping the same old Mini. For another twenty-seven years.

City Boy –The City Boy, from Upper Bavaria, was a brave 1980s attempt to reactivate flagging interest in the micro car.

When this photo was taken in 1983, Adalbert W. Fries had built just six examples, almost entirely by hand. He'd obviously been such a busy Herr, he'd lacked time to tell his twenty-year-old daughter, Doris (pictured), that the City Boy had an engine and didn't need to be carried by hand.

A two-seater, it was 2.1 metres long and weighed 168 kilograms. Its 50 cc engine was good for a max speed of just 25 km/h but could achieve '4 L/100 km'.

That's an economy figure now eclipsed by real cars, but how many of those can boast the City Boy's 'polyester upholstered interior'?

Cityboy (and girl).

76 The third best-selling car of all

Well, obviously there's the VW Beetle in first position. It sold more than 21 million units between 1938 and 2003.

And obviously in second is the 15 million-plus Model T Ford, which the VW Beetle famously overtook to become champion.

Equally obviously, neither the Escort nor Corolla makes any honest list, despite claims along the way by Ford and Toyota. They are merely nameplates that have been stuck on sequences of very different cars.

So what the hell occupies the third step on the podium? The 2CV? The Mini perhaps? Could it be the Lada Riva or one of those other weird-arsed Fiat derivatives produced for decades under a string of different names behind the old Iron Curtain?

No, no, non. The bronze medal winner is the Renault R4, which sold 8,135,42 units.

Now, to many the history of Renault is only slightly more engaging than the history of corrugated cardboard packaging materials, but hear me out – it's surprisingly interesting.

The process of using pleated paper between two sheets of more rigid material was patented as a cushioning material in England in 1856, and originally used for hat boxes.

Records are made of this:
the Renault R4.

Oh hang on, this was about the R4. It was released in 1961 and stayed in production until 1992. So how did it sell so well while generally slipping under the radar (unless of course you are a Renaultphile, in which case it was probably a pulsating blip right in the centre of the screen)?

It all started during World War II, during which, as we know, France scored a golden duck with the bat, fielded appallingly, then refused to bowl until Germany's tail-enders were obviously struggling.

At stumps, the country was a basket case. Sometime during the war, however, engineers at Renault took time out from collaborating to bang up a couple of prototype models for use when peace broke out.

One of them was the 4VC, a bulbous and unstable rear-engined Beetle-copy. This was unveiled at the 1946 Paris Motor Show. As if to illustrate how austere the times were, the showcar and early production models were finished in a sand-coloured paint salvaged from Rommel's Afrika Corps.

The newly restructured Renault sold the 4CV from 1947 (the collaboration comment above wasn't a completely cheap shot; that was the reason given for its nationalisation by the French government).

Like the 2CV and Fiat Bambino, the 4CV proved just the thing for a cash-strapped, petrol-rationed Europe, and production lasted until the start of the 1960s.

At that point Renault engineers turned the design on its head. They replaced the curves with straight lines and popped the engine up front, driving the front wheels. They stuck a hatchback on the tail too.

It was the all-new R4 and, although VW aficionados will argue in favour of the 1970s Golf, the Renault might be the world's first modern front-drive hatch.

The R4 was assembled in Australia for many years, and (like the 4CV) was popular with the new wave of European migrants who didn't fall for the 'big car for a big country' spin. *What for you need all those cylinders?*

To enhance its Frenchness, Australian buyers were offered a 'Parisienne' model with canework on the sides of the bodywork.

In many parts of the world, the R4 lasted through the 1970s and 1980s, by which time its antiquated production methods made it comparatively expensive to build.

In 1992, the last thousand R4s were produced. They were badged as the 'Bye Bye', a French expression meaning 'bye bye'.

Even then, in a couple of countries they kept knocking together examples from existing parts into the mid-1990s, meaning the R4 was one of the longest-lived models as well.

So now you know. Just tell me you care.

77 Which car should Janet buy?

The dilemma

Janet is the proprietor of a successful mid-sized import–export business and an enthusiastic driver. She wants a roadster or small coupe (she has no children) but, running a company with a strong commitment to the environment, she puts high store on fuel efficiency and low emissions. She'd prefer a prestige European brand and can spend up to $120,000.

Our advice

Well, Janet, we have a bit to work through here. Some advice columns would merely take your requirements on face value, then spit out some shallow advice based on a bit of real-world experience and a few of their own prejudices.

We're much more thorough than that here.

That's why we've had a private detective follow you this past month, listening in on your phone calls, reading your emails and Tasering your boyfriend.

Yes, that was us. Many apologies, but your Steve found us looking over the fence with night-vision binoculars and, you have to admit, that pea-brained hulk can be pretty damn threatening.

As always, our commitment is to calculating exactly what is right for you, rather than what you merely think is right. That's why we also hacked your bank statements, put the forensic auditors through your company and interviewed your friends and family while disguised as police officers.

First, let's look at a few sub-$120,000 Euro sportsters. There's the Porsche Boxster, of course, and the BMW Z4. You can just about squeeze a 35is version of the Z4 into your budget but the cheaper and more frugal 20i may fit the stated requirements better. There's the Audi TT too, in a variety of engine configurations, and the Benz SLK. However, we're loath to suggest any, for reasons we'll come to shortly.

Firstly, we need to talk about environmental efficiency. Why care about your car's emissions, when your company – we'd call it small, not 'mid-sized', btw – doesn't give a rat's about where it sources stuff? You'd switch suppliers to save half a cent a unit.

Don't misunderstand. It's surprising what high-quality brackets and hinges North Korean political prisoners can make in a freezing cellar, while up to their knees in chemical waste. But we can't help feeling you're not being honest with us, or yourself, when stating your 'green' motoring requirements.

And what's with the 'import–export' corporate description? The only things you export are Australian dollars.

Enthusiastic driver? The tracker we've had placed under your current car suggests otherwise. Unless you drive slowly and inattentively *with great enthusiasm*. Most importantly, where the hell are you going to get $120,000, unless you have a second set of books to show the money-lenders?

Steve thinks you own the house. And the work premises. He hasn't read the 'pay your rent or get out' letters that we've carefully perused. Mind you, he's in the dark about the car insurance fraud convictions too. And the shoplifting. Same with the last bloke. Ask yourself why you can't hold on to a man, Janet. Why you have no children …

Anyway, as always we aim to give our correspondents honest, helpful advice. So here it is: you can't afford a new car and you are delusional about your company, which is neither eco nor successful.

That's why we have two recommendations. The first is to stick with the heavily dented Holden Barina you are currently driving (but have the damn thing serviced – it's been two years!).

Our other recommendation concerns the money transfer you initiated last year to hide the proceeds of the only winning deal you've closed since 2009. That's a recommendation we'll forward directly to the tax department and corporate regulators. No doubt you'll hear from them soon.

Hope we've sorted out your dilemma. Who else would have gone to so much trouble?

78 Is this really the standard of the world?

After American Football's Super Bowl in 2012, some flip attached to the New York Giants – a coach or manager, I think – was being interviewed about what it was like for him and his team to be *world* champions.

He explained with no sense of irony (or geography) that the simple reason his team were champions *of the world* was because they had the best players *in the world*.

That's one of the many things we find fascinating about Americans – their childlike self-centredness. And the belief that when New York beats Boston in a game that brings together helmets and ballet tights, and is taken seriously in no other nation, that makes New York the world champions.

You wonder whose idea it was to give them their own country, don't you.

Anyway, in the same spirit, Cadillac traded for a century on the slogan 'Standard of the World.' It was a line picked up in 1908 when the company won the prestigious Dewar Trophy for excellence in manufacturing.

That Trophy was awarded for parts interchangeability; Cadillac tolerances were proven to be so fine that three cars could be stripped down, their parts mingled and then the three cars rebuilt.

That was progress in 1908, but the company persisted with the slogan, even when its cars were light years behind Europe and Asia in quality, engineering and aesthetics (similar things could be said about Rolls 'Best Car in the World' Royce, but let's not confuse the narrative).

Lately, Cadillac has added the word 'new' to the slogan, though not as in 'Standard of the New World', which might be grimly accurate. Instead, since 2010 it has been 'Cadillac, New Standard of the World.'

The tagline now implies the company has jumped a level higher again, further humbling that largely unexplored place known as 'Everywhere else.'

Now let's not be too harsh on poor old Caddie. It can't be much fun re-skinning ugly Chevrolets and trying to make them look premium.

And it can't be easy building and selling 2.5-tonne body-on-frame Escalade SUVs while trying to convince yourself you are bringing good into the world. (By the way, the GM bumf says the Escalade is the standard by which all other luxury SUVs are measured. This is probably true, as in 'Compared with an Escalade, ours is 60 per cent lighter, 70 per cent more fuel efficient, 80 per cent more refined and 90 per cent safer.')

Looking at today's bloated, unimaginative, parts-bin Caddies, it can be easy to overlook that these guys once really did lead the way in some areas. The company was either first or very early with the electric starter, the enclosed body, synchromesh gears and even airbags. There was a lot of gimmicky and not-quite-there stuff in the 1950s and 1960s such as headlights that automatically turned on and off (and even self-dimmed), climate control air-con, electrically warmed seats and cruise

1954 La Espada.

control. But they were certainly giving it a go.

For sheer bombast, the company produced a V16 in 1930 and, later, an 8.2-litre V8, eclipsing the capacity of even the V16 (which peaked at 7.4 litres). Take that, world! The Caddie also introduced automotive tailfins, inspired by jet engines and dagmar bumpers, inspired by Dagmar, the pneumatic American TV actress. Both features have gone on to save so many lives …

1956 Eldorado Evolution.

From the 1970s it was just a case of limping along, hoping to get away with it. That could be why the Cadillac badge has laurels on it. The company has to rest on something.

Maybe one day it will again produce world-beating cars. And the Nigerian Patriots will beat the Swedish Redskins in the Super Bowl.

79 Here's how they do it

Today's cars can be ludicrously frugal. The VW Golf BlueMotion, for example, is capable of sipping just 3.8 litres of petrol every 100 kilometres. It emits a mere 99 grams of carbon for each k driven – from an everyday 1.6-litre turbo-diesel.

To check it wasn't hype, I took to the road and discovered if I breathed in and didn't use the air-conditioning or headlights, I could match and even better those officially laboratory-derived consumption

figures. But it left the question: how do they do it? How are car companies achieving such numbers – the sort they argued only a few years ago were completely impossible? It could only be by using some pretty out-there secret technology. Such as, just perhaps …

Supressed inventions – Could it be that the miracle carburettor, the patents of which were bought up long ago by fuel companies, carmakers and the Provisional One World Government, have finally been pressed into service? Not fully, of course, because we all know that 240 miles per gallon, or 1.18 L/100 km, was achieved by one of the cars that accidentally slipped out of the GM factory in the 1960s. It's possible carmakers will slowly introduce as much of this suppressed technology as necessary, after striking a deal whereby the oil companies will increase the price of fuel at exactly the rate people are saving it.

Fuel additives – Although considered by some to be a complete scam, research on the Internet shows many excellent products available, some of them in convenient-to-take capsule form. They can reduce toxic fumes by 90 per cent (guaranteed) and improve fuel economy by a third (otherwise your money, sent overseas to a company listing no physical address, will be returned immediately). For example, the addition of just 45 millilitres of 'Miracle Miles' fluid to each tank will lift mileage by 15 to 25 per cent, thanks to Advanced Radionics.* It's reasonable to suspect the VW and other modern fuel sippers automatically insert such a product into their fuel as they drive.

Perpetual motion – Although closed-minded types argue perpetual motion machines violate the laws of thermodynamics, enlightened people, er, don't. The Discovery Channel's *Future Cars* raised the possibility that the French MDI compressed-air car could have an on-board generator that could squeeze its air, and this in turn could push the car forward and repower the generator so it could squeeze more air …

OK, I struggled to follow how this could go on *ad infinitum*, but I don't work in television. The promise, though, was we'd never fill up 'ever, and with not an iota of pollution … ever'. It's

otherwise possible the BlueMotion VW has one of those pivoting drinking birds under its mystical bonnet, connected to a cog that feeds into the batteries.

Water injection – As we've discussed, only loons think an engine will run solely on water. You need to mix it with petrol first! Aquatune water injection systems offer 25 per cent better mileage and up to 30 per cent more power.

Cynics will say coating your exhaust with peanut butter also gives 'up to' 30 per cent more power (a range that obviously includes zero), but what about Aquatune's proven fuel economy gains? Or the complete elimination of turbo lag, improved longevity (for the engine, not you) and other absolutely guaranteed advantages?

The Aquatune device atomises the water and air that goes into the engine 'where it is further atomized [and] collides with the fuel molecules making a highly explosive mixture and expanding the fuel. As this mixture goes into the combustion chamber a marvellous thing happens – a chain reaction … making in essence a half steam engine, half gas engine.'

It's amazing that none of the world's carmakers have heartily embraced such technology (until now of course). Another advantage: Aquatune won't harm the engine 'even if you run out of water'.

* What are Radionics? According to the Miracle Miles website: 'In the mid-20th century, Dr Thomas Galen Hieronymus theorized that Radionics – the application of radio frequencies to enhance human biology – could be used on inanimate matter. To test his hypothesis, Hieronymus attempted to fertilize a whole farm with only the electronic signature of fertilizer and discovered that the agricultural matter on the property was positively affected. Miracle Miles has followed in the footsteps of the pioneering Dr. Hieronymus, utilizing his theories of Radionics to produce an advanced gas additive …'

Don't delay, order today.

80 Carmakers no one's heard of: the incomplete list

Obviously there can't be carmakers absolutely no one has heard of. Someone has to turn on the factory lights each day, so you can assume at least one person knows that such concerns as Breckland, Devon and Donkervoot exist.

So what are the really obscure car companies? Well Etox, for starters. It aims to be a Turkish delighter of sports-car aficionados, but so far the Ankara-based company hasn't exactly set the world alight. It hasn't even started a spot fire.

Its Zafer coupe is an interesting-looking thing, though the aggressive styling rather overstates the performance it wrings out of its 1.5-litre diesel. The official 0–100 km/h time is 13 seconds.

Turkey's Etox.

Donkervoort D8GT.

If you're not about to go into Etox, consider the Fulgara Laraki. It's a sophisticated-looking sportster with scissor doors and a blend of Lamborghini and Benz parts. And it's built in Morocco. Yes, Morocco, down Casablanca way.

The Laraki's supercar claims are supported by a 686 kW Mercedes V12 engine. Unfortunately the guy that turns the lights on each day doesn't seem to be answering his phone at the moment.

The Artega GT sports car started life as a German project and was unveiled just in time for the GFC. Which was not ideal. The company was then bought out by a Mexican businesswoman and beer heiress with a name slightly longer than a Maybach 62: María Asunción Aramburuzabala Larregui de Garza. There has been at least one confirmed Artega order. Who knows, one day there could be another.

The British Isles has always been a welcoming home for eccentrics. It's there you'll find such things as the Breckland Beira V8, a British car based on GM's Saturn platform. Considering that Saturn went supernova in the GFC, let's hope Breckland bought a few platforms in advance. Though with the Beira wearing a $120,000 price tag, let's hope not too many.

One car that doesn't come from England, despite the name, is the Devon. Did someone once look at their packed school lunch and say, 'now there's a good name for a car'? The Devon GTX is set to be the next American supercar. Say the builders. Sorry, was that me yawning?

The Devon is one of those cars that look beautiful from some angles and are best not viewed from others. Production is limited to thirty-five units, probably by demand.

And there's Donkervoot. It's as Dutch as salted liquorice and looks like a Caterham 7 Clubman looks after you've spent a couple of hours under dentist's gas.

Hongqi is known as the Chinese Rolls-Royce, not because of its quietness, refinement and benchmark quality, but because it keeps building ludicrous copies of Rollers with even bigger grilles than the originals. Hongqi is older than most Chinese car companies, building big black limousines for communist party bosses from the 1950s.

Hongqi has made various other oddities though the years including an Audi 100 four-door … convertible. No shit. Of course we could rave on about obscure Chinese car brands, but millions and millions of Chinese have heard of some of them – and it won't be too long before several of the brands become household names here. Hongqi probably won't be one of them.

Germany's Isdera is yet another supercar maker. For sheer weirdness, check out its Autobahnkurier AK116i, a retro-bizarre coupe with VW Beetle doors and two Benz V8s – one at each end.

Isdera is rather secretive. One report says the company has sold seventy cars, but considering it was started in 1969, it's possible there are just one or two buyers, who update every year.

Some small car companies opt for names that will ensure they stay small. Like Farbio. One shouldn't be too shallow about names and, anyway, the British-built Farbio GTS is almost attractive enough to overcome its daft handle. But it's also built on the blue-sky optimism that propels so many small carmakers: the idea that people will pay Porsche or Ferrari money for something that is neither. You've bought a what? A Farbio? Tell me it isn't so.

How about a Tramontana? It's a Spanish attempt to make a road-registerable Formula One car, complete with outboarder wheels,

The bizarre Isdera Autobahnkurier.

impossibly low nose wing and an inability to manage even a small-scale replica of a speed bump. One or two seats can be shoehorned into the carbon fibre/aluminium tub. The maker insists production will be limited to no more than twelve vehicles a year. With a price exceeding €385,000, it certainly will be.

Covini has spent about three decades trying to make six-wheeled cars fashionable. The C6W – now in 'limited production' – looks like a conventional mid-engined sports car that's been badly photoshopped. The second set of wheels is upfront and the arch that accommodates them takes a big bite out of the doors.

Proto Motors is South Korea's answer to another question that may never be asked. Its scissor-doored Spirra coupe can reputedly top 300 km/h. But why buy a Korean supercar you've never heard of when you can buy a wide variety of American and European ones you never will hear of?

Such as the Caparo, a Tramontana-like racer for the road with outrageous bodywork and price. Or the American Saleen S7 with claimed zero to 100 km/h time of 2.8 seconds (stop me if you've heard that before) and enough grilles, louvres and NACA ducts to cube, grate and julienne a barn full of vegetables.

Italy's F&M Auto Vulca is extravagantly styled, to use a euphemism. F&M stands for Faralli and Mazzanti, two blokes otherwise known as Mario and Rossello, who say 'Vulca will be produced in very limited numbers: only ten, individually numbered. This will ensure exclusivity ...'

Not wrong there. You can apparently stay at their Tuscan villa and supervise the building of your car. Well, why not?

81 Aren't car blogs terrific?

❝ I've been thinking lately how interesting it is that most cars have four wheels. Well, five, if you count the spare wheel. Though not all cars have those nowadays. There's the steering wheel too, I guess. Anyway, that's it for today. **❞**

Great post, love your work. But you should have mentioned most Holdens only have two or three wheels cause Holdens are crap and they fall off.
Posted by: Henry Forever/Sydney

TL:DR ['too long didn't read']
Posted by: Bored civil servant/Anywhere

I say, my car has 21 inch wheels and hubcaps that keep the badge always pointing upright. What ho.
Posted by: Roller Boy/Brisbane

Henry Forever is talking rubbish again. Bet he doesn't realise that 100 per cent of Falcons were built by child abusers.
Posted by: Com Adorer/Melbourne

Says who?
Posted by: Henry Forever/Sydney

Says everyone. Check Dikipedia.
Posted by: Com Adorer/Melbourne

Maybe we could keep it a spot less personal.
Posted by: Roller Boy/Brisbane

Shut up, moron idiot gitbreath.
Posted by: Henry Forever/Sydney

Yeah, you pickled goose stuffed shirt know-nothing.
Posted by: Com Adorer/Melbourne

Are you sure that's less personal?
Posted by: Roller Boy/Brisbane

Checked Wikipedia, HF. Says Holdens are the car of choice of [comment deleted by moderator].
Posted by: Henry Forever/Sydney

As this is supposed to be about wheels, can I just mention something about wheels? Like ask why do we still measure them in inches?
Posted by: Ken/Adelaide

Go find your own forum.
Posted by: Antisocial networker/Darwin

Re wheels: we don't really measure them. We just read the size off the pack.
Posted by: Valvegrinder/Perth

I think it's something to do with Americans. They still use cubits as well.
Posted by: Ken/Adelaide

The fastest car ever built was the Thrust SSC. That had three wheels. And the back ones steered.
Posted by: Speed Demon/Melbourne

How gay. Can we go back to what a wombat Com Adorer is?
Posted by: Henry Forever/Sydney

Did it have a spare, or just one of those tubes of gunk.
Posted by: Valvegrinder/Perth

The Thrust? Don't know. Don't think space savers are rated to travel above the speed of sound.
Posted by: Speed Demon/Melbourne

Can't be true. They have them in Hyundais.
Posted by: Accentman/Darwin

No they don't.
Posted by: Expert on everything/Sydney

A car is not having proper spare wheels anymore – why was I not told?
Posted by: Toomas/Estonia

[Comment about the intimate habits of Ford owners deleted by moderator.]
Posted by: Com Adorer/Melbourne.

[Comment about the intimate habits of mothers of Commodore owners deleted by moderator, now blushing severely.]
Posted by: Henry Forever/Sydney.

There was a Wolseley thing that had just two wheels and used a gyroscope. Would have been even more interesting if it really worked.
Posted by: Valvegrinder/Perth

The Holden version would have worked.
Posted by: Com Adorer/Melbourne

What about Mitsubishis?
Posted by: Zero Hero/Bathurst

Oh god you're back.
Posted by: Antisocial networker/Darwin

Well I had a compulsory OH&S keyboard break to complete. Then it was lunch.
Posted by: Zero Hero/Bathurst

Yeah, we just had a 4-hour HR presentation on efficiency.
Posted by: Ken/Adelaide

The Fuoco has three wheels too.
Posted by: Valvegrinder/Perth

Get Fuoco'd.
Posted by: Antisocial networker/Darwin

Get Fuoco'd ... LOL. At last, someone who speaks English.
Posted by: Speed Demon/Melbourne

Why or when is a Fuoco?
Posted by: Toomas/Estonia

It's a motorbike, dimwit.
Posted by: Com Adorer/Melbourne

Oops, 5 o'clock got to go.
Posted by: Bored civil servant/Anywhere

Me too.
Posted by: Everyone else/Everywhere

Discussion finished. Thanks for another fascinating and robust conversation about wheels. See you back at 9am.
Moderator.

82 Ticking the historic boxes

There it was, parked on the side of a normal suburban street: a 1976 Chrysler Galant officially registered as a Historic Vehicle.

I don't wish to be unkind to Galant owners – heaven knows they're hard enough on themselves – but I'm still struggling to come to grips with this disturbing sight.

How could a government agency make such a landmark decision without, well, without consulting you or me?

What pen-pushing, slightly agoraphobic, stained shirted, mother-fixated civil servant saw the application form and confidently said, 'Yep, the 1976 Chrysler Galant – that ticks all the historic boxes'?

And what, for him, was the deciding factor? Was it the classically nondescript three-box sedan styling? Or perhaps the panache with which Chrysler Australia stuck its own badges – in turn borrowed from the US – on an out-of-the-box Mitsubishi?

Maybe it was the performance and handling that once saw a Galant qualify fifty-ninth in the annual Bathurst enduro. And then fail to finish.

Or perchance the granting of the 'historic' imprimatur was a direct response to the technical specifications. As Galant aficionados – all three of them – will tell you, these included a carburettored four-cylinder engine optimistically claimed as developing 75 kW, a live rear axle and rear drum brakes.

For collectors only: the Galant.

So intense was my need to know more, it led me from Google to, well, Google. Along the way I discovered not only how to whiten my teeth and meet Asian women in my area, but that the official definition of 'historic', at least as far as motor cars are concerned, is 'slightly old'.

In New South Wales, vehicles manufactured thirty or more years ago are eligible for historic registration, providing 'the operator belongs to an RTA-recognised historic vehicle club, and the vehicle has not been altered except for certain safety features or period accessories'. The VicRoads club permit scheme specifies twenty-five years rather than thirty.

There are several worries here, the first being that there is no need for the vehicle to be revolutionary, significant or even appealing. You and I now live in a world where a Morris Marina is a historic vehicle. Yes, a Marina – that woefully badly designed mechanical affront, half-heartedly bolted together in Australia by a company listed in the dictionary under 'ailing'.

A Datsun 120Y too. Yes, a One-bloody-twenty-bloody-Y! And it's all on seniority, no merit required. Declaring a Datsun 120Y as a historic vehicle solely because it was built before a certain date is rather like saying a rhyme-less, metre-free, meaningless assemblage of words is a poem, just because it was published in *The Australian Literary Review*.

Another worrying thing lies in the proof. The authorities will accept that your vehicle is historic as long as you can find other people who agree with you, that is people who are prepared to let you into their club. But what sort of individuals would these be? Who would be in Galant, Marina or 120Y enthusiasts' association? And if you'd been charged with a crime, would you want them on your jury? Not very likely.

There's another side to this argument and, being equal opportunity enthusiasts, we'll give it: One man's Galant sedan with vinyl roof is another's Mercedes Benz 300SL gullwing coupe. One woman's 1975 Datsun 120Y is another's 1967 Toyota 2000GT.

One transgender person's Marina Six is another transgender person's Lamborghini Mi … no, I can't even finish that sentence. Any Marina is an insult to every sentient being.

But you get the general drift. As soon as governments start making aesthetic judgements about which cars are significant and which are not, then we are well on the way to being a police state. Therefore, it's much safer for democracy to leave such fundamental decisions to pen-pushing, slightly agoraphobic, stained shirted, mother-fixated civil servants.

Holden Camira: your moment is nigh!

83 Final four-wheeled falsehoods

OK, just a few more examples that prove that untruth is stranger than fiction:

- In 1962 Chrysler introduced the first car with a day–night rear-view mirror. The mirror had been developed by NASA in case the Mercury-manned spaceship was followed by an alien craft with its lights on high beam.

- The downgrading of St Christopher, holy protector of travellers, leaves us with only two motoring-related beatified persons: (a) Petraeus, patron saint of fuel injection, and (b) Berryl the Lesser, the matron saint of rear legroom.

- Several potential Bathurst-winning muscle cars were quashed in the face of political pressure in the years directly after the so-called supercar scare of 1972. One such car, the Falcon GT-HO Phase 5.1, would have been the first Falcon with full surround sound.

- Despite being widely quoted as saying 'Whatever is rightly done, however humble, is noble,' car-builder Henry Royce later admitted that his original sentence was 'Whatever is rightly done … is nobbled.' This was because his partner Charles Rolls was an early advocate of HR and OH&S. Henry couldn't pick up a spanner without filling out a form in triplicate. Whenever he wanted to get something done, he found himself instead attending courses on Maximising Productivity in the Workplace. The original plan was to compete with the Ford T, but only a few hundred Rolls-Royces could be built each year.

- M.A.F.L., or Motorised Australian Football League, is now the highest rating televised sport in Lithuania. For those unfamiliar: it is based on Aussie Rules, but with the players driving Lada Nivas. The sport requires a field so large most games are played between the runways on Vilnius's recently completed Warwick Capper International Airport.

- In 2009 Professor Primly Rogers won a Pulitzer Prize for *Manual Excitement: A social history of the single-clutch gearbox in the Americas.*

- Cyclist Lance Armstrong has two famous relatives with connections in the car world. The first was Sir William George Armstrong, the British industrialist whose company merged to form the Armstrong-Siddeley car and aircraft engine concern in 1919. He was found to regularly inject EPO, but escaped sanctions. The second was Neil Armstrong, the American astronaut who fronted a series of car commercials for Chrysler. He was eventually charged with faking seven moon landings and banned for life from astronauting.

- Most Lamborghini model names are drawn from bull-fighting, such as Miura (a fierce breed of bull), Espada (the sword used for the coup de grace) and of course Murciélago, named after the manoeuvre where a bull avenges its public torture by using its last breath to fatally gore the matador through the groin.

84 The black test car

What is that mysterious shrouded motor car?

It's the prototype Tiger Pioneer, that's what it is. And it's from a truly offbeat Japanese film entitled *Black Test Car*.

This black-and-white effort from 1962 was promoted as 'the first thriller about salaried workers'. How could anyone resist?

It was made by one Yasuzo Masumura, a man responsible for a series of films satirising both Japanese industry and his compatriots' obsession with consumerism and Westernisation.

Black Test Car begins with ominous music as Tiger Corporation engineers begin the 'high speed test' for their new Pioneer.

The car has been covered in black canvas and beefed up to look like a standard family model, despite it being a secret sports machine.

As an executive explains in one of the boardroom meetings: 'People want speed and luxury! Sports cars deliver both.' Alas, Tiger's prototype didn't deliver either. Soon into the test, the new coupe (well, a model of it only slightly more convincing than the original Godzilla) flies off the road and bursts into flames.

STARRING JIRO TAMIYA   JUNKO KANO   EIJI FUNAKOSHI   HIDEO TAKAMATSU
MUSIC SEI IKENO   CINEMATOGRAPHY YOSHIHISA NAKAGAWA
SCREENPLAY BY KAZUO FUNABASHI   YOSHIHIRO ISHMATSU
ORIGINAL STORY BY SUEYUKI KAJIYAMA
DIRECTED BY YASUZO MASUMURA

The suggestion that this might indicate a safety problem is not enough to delay production.

Soon it becomes obvious that Tiger and its Pioneer are being spied on by agents of rival carmaker Yamato.

Tiger decides to counter with its own program of espionage, misinformation, blackmailing, bribery, kidnapping, prostituting and violence. The only time the film strains credibility is with the suggestion journalists might be unethical too.

And what do stolen blueprints reveal? Yamato has nicked the Pioneer design and is rushing to market an almost identical coupe called Mypet.

The DVD version includes a nicely remastered print of the film and a small booklet written in that dense, film-critic style that almost requires you to put up a base camp before attempting the first sentence.

The background info reveals that, although Masumura might have specialised in pillorying Japanese industry, he shared its efficiency. *Black Test Car* was his twenty-first feature film for Daiei Studios, and one of three he made during 1962.

It's obviously low budget, and pure film noir, with heavy shadows and spy-like camera angles from above, below or peering through openings.

Once it's known the two sports cars will be hitting the market at the same time, the challenge is for Tiger to surreptitiously discover what Yamato will be charging, so it can undercut the Mypet (which is not to be confused with the film's rather cool Toyopet, an early Crown sedan with suicide rear doors used in a kidnapping scene).

When we have a chance to see both cars unmasked, it becomes obvious the role of Pioneer is played by a very lightly modified Renault Caravelle hardtop. The Mypet appears to be an even less changed VW Karmann Ghia coupe.

There isn't a great deal of footage of moving cars, however; this is the backroom story. Where there are cars, there are continuity problems. When a Pioneer is pushed in front of a train (as part of the general chicanery), the wreck clearly has four doors.

One executive, Asahina, has a moral epiphany at the end, and throws his corporate badge on the floor – an act far more significant in Japan than most countries.

The general message is that all companies are evil, every employee can be corrupted, all human decency is left behind in the march towards 'progress' and we're all going to die a horrible death. We won't die this horrible death, though, before we've sent our fiancées to bed rival executives so they can steal industrial secrets, and have yelled at the top of our voices that anything is permissible 'As long as we win!'

Nothing wrong with a bit of realism, now is there?

85 When cars and smoke go together

In the 1990s, Fairfax columnist Paddy McGuinness wrote that the car industry 'while producing a lethal product has escaped much of the moralistic censure directed against the tobacco industry'. Much later the actor (and bicycle advocate) Matthew Modine went a step further – quite a big step really.

'The sexy lifestyle that the tobacco industry sold to us,' Modine fumed (if that's the right word) in *The Huffington Post*, 'contains the same advertising lies and poison which the automobile industry sold and continues to sell to the world.

'Just as tobacco has killed millions with different forms of cancer, the automobile industry … must be looked upon as a carton of cigarettes and a cancer to civilization.'

Some may think these comments are hard but fair. Others might say they are as loopy as something so loopy it makes for an effective and slightly amusing metaphor.

People have suggested warning labels for cars, but not plain packaging, so far. 'No, I'm sorry, sexy styling is out. From today all cars will be olive and shaped like Soviet Bloc Skodas.'

Without weighing into cigarette–carmaker moral equivalency, it's

fair to say that people in general are very hard on cigarette companies. It's a shame because Big Tobacco has done so much for cars and motoring. Like, er...

- The Falcon GT came about because of cigarettes, sort of. The object was to win 1967's Gallaher 500 at Bathurst, a motor sport enduro selflessly underwritten by the Gallaher tobacco company. Although most original GTs were gold, Ford Australia produced special silver examples for ciggie company reps by way of thankyou. Classic after classic GT followed.
- Cigarette lighters are highly useful power sources for small devices, and we'd probably never have them if not for smoking. Some

carmakers of the 1960s and 1970s, such as Cadillac, were so keen to power such devices they included four or more lighters.

- Durries have provided that cool, satisfying taste for many in motor sport, whether Keke Rosberg or the young Peter Brock lighting up on the podium, or Dick Trickle smoking during a race. The NASCAR driver, whose name guaranteed a mention no matter where he finished, drilled a hole in his helmet to make it possible. In keeping with his deep interest in occupational health and safety, though, Trickle puffed away only during yellow flag car periods.

- Smoking made racing safer. From 1968, when advertising was allowed on F1 cars, big tobacco used its clout to help clean up a sport only slightly safer than ritual slaughter. Cynics will say

Gold Leaf and others didn't want their glamorous ambassadors immolated in public only for fear of damaging their brands. But that's the thing about cynics – they're so cynical.

- Statistically, gasper manufacturers have made road cars safer too, by directly contributing to five of the diseases that have helped push traffic accidents down to tenth in the World Health Organization's list of causes of death.

- Despite an advertising ban, Marlboro has been so big-hearted it has continued to sponsor the Ferrari F1 team without thought of gain or recognition. It seems only good manners that, in return, Ferrari paints up its race-cars to gently remind people of that company and all the good it has done.

- Fag packets have given us the coolest race-car paint schemes, such as the black and gold used for JPS Lotus. This has been revived recently, not to make people take up smoking, we're sure. Perhaps not even to make them change brands, but simply because it looks classy. Some Lotus road cars have been painted that way too.

OK, on balance it's not a lot. Just as well then that Big Tobacco's on the back foot and motorsport, for example, can be underwritten by alcohol and gambling instead.

BASED ON A TRUE STORY

86 Obituary: Lord Stanley Oversteer

Motoring pioneer Lord Stanley Oversteer has died at the age of 101.

Although best known for giving his surname to the practice of hanging out the tail, Oversteer had an improbably long and fascinating career in motor sport.

Sir Laurance Ponceby mused in his *Encyclopaedia of Titled Racing Drivers*: 'If Stirling Moss was the greatest Grand Prix pilot never to be World Champion, surely Oversteer was the greatest never to finish a race.'

In 603 starts, he came close many times. In Monaco, 1932, Oversteer famously ran out of fuel on the first lap and had his servants push his car across the line – fifty-two times. He was still judged a 'non-finisher', however, on a technicality relating to the servants' dress code.

Born in Frumley-on-Old-Money in 1909, Oversteer was the eldest son of the Third Earl of Berkeley Hunt. He was sent to Eton then Oxford then Brooklands, where he found his metier, first as a riding mechanic prized for his lightness, then as the driver of a series of aero-engined specials, prized for his tail-happy technique and fearless stupidity.

His double, triple and, on one occasion, quad-engined specials were widely judged too powerful, tearing themselves – and Oversteer

– to shreds. When the third version of his twenty-seven-cylinder aero-engined Flippy Floppy Pip Pop was fitted with ribbed steel tyres, it dug a hole in the Brooklands track so deep it was later used as an underground fuel depot.

Curiously, it was in a hot-air balloon where Oversteer came closest to losing his life. His crash into an empty croquet field in 1937 killed two scantily clad chambermaids and his most prized racehorse. The former led to a scandal, the latter to much head-scratching.

Oversteer recovered by World War II and led the Grand Prix Espionage unit, charged with ensuring Britain was immediately competitive when hostilities ceased. At one stage he smuggled a complete eight-cylinder Mercedes W125 engine out of Germany in his underpants. Shortly before D-Day, he was captured and tortured in France, but Oversteer refused to give up English axle ratios or engine firing orders.

When the modern F1 championship started in 1950, Oversteer failed

Early, tail-happy days.

to secure a works drive. Instead he built his own monoposto based around the Austin A40 Dorset. He managed to lead the first lap of every GP in 1950 and 1951, without once completing the second.

He later reflected that the Dorset's 1.2-litre straight four, modified to achieve a one-hundred-to-one compression ratio, may have been overtaxed keeping up with the 350 bhp-plus supercharged Alfas. After one engine failure, the cylinder head was found 18 miles away.

Oversteer lost the family fortune in the 1960s in a doomed attempt to set up a US sales operation for the Dago, a low-cost Eastern-Bloc sedan about which the name was not even the most unfortunate thing.

He returned to prosperity in the 1970s as executive producer of a series of 8 mm films starring his seventh wife, known simply as Kitten. This financed another Formula One foray; at sixty-three Oversteer was the oldest in the field and preserved his perfect non-finishing record.

Ground effects F1 cars aggravated his arthritis, so Oversteer turned to production racing, breaking down and/or crashing at every UK circuit before repeating the feat in various European championships. His only Bathurst 1000 attempt, at the age of seventy-two, ended when scrutineers discovered a Rolls-Royce Conway turbofan jet engine under the bonnet of his ten-year-old Triumph Dolomite.

Last Tuesday Oversteer's life was cruelly cut short when he engaged first gear accidentally during high-speed engine testing of the forty-eight-cylinder Bugatti Veyron special he was building on the second floor of his Suffolk manor house.

He is survived by his estranged wife Esmeralda (twenty-three), his favourite hunting dogs and a small coterie of young and impeccably well-groomed Sicilian men. We shall not see his like again.

87 More questions for the cranially retentive

1. What Japanese car company takes its name from the supreme deity of the ancient Persian religion of Zoroastrianism?

2. What were the first names of the men who gave their names to the following brands of car: Chrysler, Benz, Citroën and Honda?

3. A Porsche coupe of the early 1960s was to be known as the 901 model – until it was discovered that another European company had registered all the three-number automotive model designations with a zero in the middle. What was the company that indirectly led to the Porsche 901 being renamed the 911?

4. What car answers to this description? Maximum power: 43 kW at 12,500 rpm. Engine capacity: 600 cc. Suspension: four-wheel independent. Drive system: rear wheels, by chain.

5. What popular small(ish) car – sold in Australia since the 1960s – is named after the collective term for the inner petals of a flower?

6. Who is the only South African (so far) to win the Formula One World Championship. For two extra entirely meaningless points: what year, what team?

7. What fifty-year-old badge did Chevrolet reintroduce with the seventh generation Corvette in 2013?

8. The first full-length feature film by Australian director Peter Weir, which dates to 1974, was released in America as *The Cars That Eat People*. What was its Australian title?

9. In what countries would you find the following race circuits: Estoril, Spa-Francorchamps, Suzuka, The Nurburgring?

10. What notable – but controversial – Australian car won the *Wheels* magazine 'Car of the Year' award for 1973.

NB: Answers are on page 319.

88 Answers to the quizzes

Test your knowledge and amaze your friends (or not) (page 91)

1. False. It is not true that Mitsubishi Australia had more 380 sedans returned under its 'Bring it back if you're not completely satisfied' policy than were sold. The 380 was a sales dud, but not quite that much of a sales dud. It was on the market between 2005 and 2008.

2. True. While honouring automotive pioneer Ransom Eli Olds by naming the Interstate 496 the R.E. Olds Freeway, Michigan authorities flattened his historic mansion so the road could pass through.

3. False. Enzo Ferrari's nephew was not christened F259 Guido Ferrari.

4. True. The first concept car from the VW-owned Bugatti concern was the EB118 show-car, unveiled at the 1998 Paris Motor Show. It was powered by a 6.3-litre 'W18', comprised of three banks of six cylinders.

5. True. Henry Ford did narrowly miss out on the US senate in 1918. He was beaten by Truman H. Newberry. Incidentally, another politician, Adolf Hitler, was one of Ford's biggest fans during the 1920s. Despite having a limited interest in cars (apart from the VW in the 1930s), young Adolf not only had a portrait of Henry on his wall, he also gave the carmaker the honour of being the only American mentioned in *Mein Kampf*.

6. False. The Lada Samara is not built in Italy. It is built in the Russian city of Togliatti, named after an Italian communist solely to confuse people doing this quiz. Production of the Samara, briefly sold in Australia, is slated to finish at the end of 2013, after thirty years of shoddy design, appalling

manufacture and dodgy customer service.

7. True. Barry Sheene performed in Puccini's opera *Tosca* at Covent Garden alongside the legendary singers Maria Callas and Tito Gobbi, circa 1964. He was a schoolboy at the time.

8. False (surprisingly). SsangYong's Musso model in fact took its name from the Korean word for rhinoceros.

9. Almost certainly true. Reports at the time noted that when American Dan Gurney won the 1967 Le Mans 24 Hour race (with equally American co-driver A.J. Foyt) he broke all tradition and shook the winner's magnum of champagne then used it to soak Henry Ford II, various team members and surrounding journalists. Spraying the bubbly quickly became the norm.

10. True and probably false. John Cobb did break the 600-km/h mark in the 1940s. He died in a water-speed record in 1952 on Scotland's Loch Ness when he hit an unexplained wave. Some believe the cause of the wave was the secretive prehistoric beast known as 'Nessie'. Then again, some people believe the world is run by alien reptiles disguised as human beings.

Multiple choice this time (page 171)

1. (a) Tercel is the male falcon. The term is also sometimes used for the male hawk (the hawk being a name most famously used by Studebaker).

2. (a) The notorious two-stroke Lightburn Zeta was built in the same factory as power tools, car jacks and concrete-mixers.

3. (b) Malcolm Campbell's famous car was named after the play *The Bluebird* by Belgian playwright Maurice Maeterlinck.

4. (b) Kelvin, Farad and Henry are units of the SI Metric system.
5. Trick question. The Carioca was both
   (b) a streamlined Volvo car from the 1930s and
   (d) the car Preston Tucker hoped to build in Brazil after the failure of his 'Torpedo'. He was too ill to see it through.
6. (b) Craig Breedlove achieved 655.73 km/h in 1963 to set the first jet-powered World Land Speed Record. To some purists, the real record remained the 634.39 km/h that John Cobb achieved in his Railton Special, because that was a wheel-driven car.
7. (d) Legend has it that the inspiration for 'Little Red Corvette' hit the artist sometimes known as Prince while he was trying to get some sleep in a pink Edsel after a long recording session.
8. (c) Approximately 21.5 million VW Beetles were built. Or exactly 21,529,464.
9. (b) Enzo Ferrari died in 1988, aged ninety, in Maranello, Italy. Apropos of nothing much, you can now buy limited edition replicas of his famous black glasses (below).
10. (c) The Nissan Pintara takes its name from an invented word with no literal meaning. Oh, and
    (d) It's a Pintara, so who could possibly give a flying fluffy duck? It was a shockingly uninteresting vehicle.
11. (a) A Ferrari 250 Testa Rosso from 1957 fetched US$16,390,000 in 2011.

Higher prices have been paid for cars in private sales, but this set a new world record for auctions.

12. (b) Aussie race drivers Tony Gaze, Dave Walker and Paul England have all competed in World Championship Formula One races. Surviving a high-speed accident in a Morris Marina would require finding one that could travel at a high speed.

Matters Antipodean (page 247)

1. The last Australian Valiant was made during the 1980s. The final CM series was built until 1981, by which time Chrysler Australia was owned by Mitsubishi. Sales were modest but at least the car was profitable, thanks to a complete lack of expenditure on research and development.

2. Fred Astaire played the winner of 'the 1964 Australian Grand Prix at Phillip Island' in the 1959 doomsday flick *On the Beach*. Yes, the tap-dancing singer, by then sixty years old. His character kills himself shortly after winning the race. Although the film was set in Australia, the scenes of racetrack carnage were filmed not at Phillip Island but in the US. And, curiously, they involved sports cars rather than open-wheelers.

3. The 'K' in the name of the 'Australianised' Morris Mini K stood for Kangaroo. Ghastly, isn't it?

4. REDeX was marketing an upper-cylinder lubricant when it sponsored the original 'Around Australia Trials'. They were run in 1953, 1954 and 1955.

5. Ford's LTD name refers to 'Lincoln-Type Design', an internal designation that didn't stop at the factory door. Who'd want a Lincoln-type design? The only thing worse would be an actual Lincoln.

6. Bruce McLaren was the founder of the McLaren Formula One team. He was a New Zealander and in December 1959 became the youngest driver

to win a Grand Prix. He was twenty-two years and 104 days old. His record would stand until 2003, when Fernando Alonso broke it. In 2008, Sebastian Vettel lowered it further to twenty-one years and seventy-three days. Bruce McLaren owned the team until his death in a testing accident in 1970.

7. *The F.J. Holden* was the 1977 film named after an Australian car. The theme song was sung by Frankie J. Holden, then vocalist for the band Ol' 55.

8. Jack Brabham and John Goss are the two winners of the Australian Grand Prix who have given their names to special 'sporting' versions of mass-produced Australian cars. The cars were the Brabham Torana, which was a modified and striped (but still gruesome) HB model, and the John Goss Special Falcon, which was based on an XB Hardtop.

9. The Tarago, a people mover from Toyota, shares its name with a town in New South Wales. Presumably one of the peaks in the mountain range known as The Kimberleys gave its name to the Austin Kimberley, but it hasn't been determined which one.

10. Jack Brabham, Frank Gardner, Tim Schenken, Larry Perkins and David Brabham (the youngest son of JB) have all competed in Formula One GP races in Brabham cars.

More questions for the cranially retentive (page 313)

1. Ahura Mazda was the supreme deity of Zoroastrianism before becoming a Japanese car. Ahura Mazda is considered the god of light and wisdom, which is why the name Mazda has also been used by General Electric as a brand name for incandescent bulbs.

2. The full name of the automotive magnates were Walter Chrysler, Karl

Benz, Andre Citroën and Soichiro Honda.

3. Peugeot, maker of the 205, 307, 504, 607, etc., trademarked all three-number model designations with a zero in the middle, forcing Porsche to rename its 901 model. It chose 911 instead.

4. Honda's S600 is the tiny chain-driven sportster in question. The later S800 had a conventional rear-drive system, after which Honda almost completely abandoned rear-drive for its four-wheelers until the NS-X was launched in 1990.

5. Toyota's Corolla is named after the collective term for the inner petals of a flower. No, no idea why either.

6. Jody Scheckter was the 1979 Formula One World Champion and, thus far, has been the only South African to achieve the honour. He was driving a Ferrari.

7. The seventh-generation Corvette, announced in early 2013 (but which the Americans still insist on calling the 2014 model), brought back the Stingray name, albeit as one word. It was Sting Ray when introduced with the 1963 Corvette.

8. *The Cars That Ate Paris* was the Australian name for the first full-length feature film by director Peter Weir. Paris was supposedly a town in western New South Wales.

9. The Estoril, Spa-Francorchamps, Suzuka and The Nurburgring race circuits are found in Portugal, Belgium, Japan and Germany, respectively.

10. The Leyland P76 V8 won the *Wheels* magazine 'Car of the Year' award for 1973. Amazing, isn't it?